"Deirdre, Epona and a hoot. Get ready for the real Fondis to show its face."

--Sassy Cambridge, author
"Out of the Blues"

-Cerridwen's runic response may appear cryptic but invites ancient blessings upon the writers.

"If you're lonely, and lose your hair,
Do not lose hope: Fondis is there."

--Eugene Field, author of *Poems of Childhood*

"Brilliant and lovely, containing insights of character and magic in America's rural paradise. It's obvious each piece was chosen with care: the craftsmanship is truly amazing!"

--Mountain View Ranches Homeowners Association Monthly Newsletter

"The intergalactic communications with Earth are often hazy; however, my perception of the two leggeds of Fondis grants me hope for a future with more elaborate and evolved understanding. *The Fondis Chronicles* is a must read here."

--channeled from King Basil of Sirius

"This is the best book I've chewed on in a long time."

-Minnie the Electric Sausage Jack Russell

"I came away with the singular feeling that I'd spent a long night at a tavern carousing with good friends and better drink, yet had the misfortune of not remembering a bit of it afterwards."

--Nathaniel Hawthorne, author of *Villette*

"Pretty good stuff."

--Phillip from the Fondis Bar

The Fondis Chronicles

Epona Maris,
Deirdre H. Moon
&
Roger Rural

∞
Infinity Publishing

Copyright © 2005 Joanne McLain, C.J. Prince,
& William C. Thomas

All rights reserved. No part of this book shall be reproduced or transmitted in any form or by any means, electronic, mechanical, magnetic, photographic including photocopying, recording or by any information storage and retrieval system, without prior written permission of the publisher. No patent liability is assumed with respect to the use of the information contained herein. Although every precaution has been taken in the preparation of this book, the publisher and author assume no responsibility for errors or omissions. Neither is any liability assumed for damages resulting from the use of the information contained herein.

This is a work of fiction. Names, characters, places, and incidents either are the product of the author's imagination or are used fictitiously. Any resemblance to actual events or locales or persons, living or dead, is entirely coincidental.

ISBN 0-7414-2839-3

Published by:

1094 New DeHaven Street, Suite 100
West Conshohocken, PA 19428-2713
Info@buybooksontheweb.com
www.buybooksontheweb.com
Toll-free (877) BUY BOOK
Local Phone (610) 941-9999
Fax (610) 941-9959

Printed in the United States of America
Printed on Recycled Paper
Published October 2005

DEDICATIONS

To those amazing people about whom I write.

                                                   Roger Rural

I bow down before the Muse lest she abandon me. And there I see the lips of the Goddess quiver in a smile as she guides my folly. Forever grateful am I to the Lady.

                                                              DHM

To the joyous mystery of all the life paths we have not yet danced upon.

                                                Epona Maris

ACKNOWLEDGMENTS

Endless thanks to Joanne McLain, Ph.D., whose dissertation formatting skills proved useful here, C.J. Prince, the Paragraph Queen, and William C. Thomas, bottomless fount of wit.

To Susan Monckton Fox, who has carefully, critically and courteously read every "Roger" put before her and who extended that courtesy to Deirdre and Epona. Also thanks to Karen Steinberg, Terry Vlasin and David Welch for their helpful comments.

To Thomas J. Herman, owner and publisher of *The High Plains Rider*, circulation 8,500; read throughout Douglas and Elbert Counties in Colorado, for the opportunities he has given us.

To the Elizabeth Library for tolerance of frequent giggling.

Many thanks for the gracious support of The Otherworld.

PREFACE

By Piers Pierce, D.Phils.
(University of Fondis Department of Comparative Literature)

Gentle Reader:
    This space has been intentionally left blank so you may draw your own expectations:

    This space has been intentionally left blank so you may draw your own conclusions:

CONTENTS

- Prologue 1

- ## Spring

To Begin, *EM* 5
I.   Spring Wedding, *DHM* 6
II.   The Law of Unintended Consequences, *EM* 8
III.   Adventures in Chicken Raising, *RR* 11
IV.   Exercise Interruptus, *DHM* 14
V.   In & Among Growing Things, *RR* 16
VI.   History Where You Least Expect It, *DHM* 19
VII.   A Flow of Words, *EM* 21
VIII. Sport, *RR* 23
IX.   The Mistress of Loch Fondis, *DHM* 26
X.   The Problem With Action, *RR* 28
XI.   Answers From a Treetop, *DHM* 31
XII.   A True Believer, *RR* 34

- ## Summer

Lessons in Crystal Gazing, *EM* 37
XIII.   Who I Really Am, *DHM* 39
XIV.   Fair: Honest; Decent, *RR* 41
XV.   Fondis Etiquette, *EM* 43
XVI.   An Art Book, 4-H, & the Uses of Memory, *RR* 47
XVII. Astrological Mumbo Jumbo, *DHM* 50
XVIII. The Lesson of Geese, *EM* 52

XIX.	On the Primordial Sea Floor, *RR*	56
XX.	Fourth of July, *DHM*	58
XXI.	The Language of Animals, *EM*	60
XXII.	Fashion & the Pigyard, *RR*	62
XXIII.	Pierced, *DHM*	66
XXIV.	Building On Our Differences, *EM*	68
XXV.	Lughnassa Festivities, *DHM*	70
XXVI.	Obstacle Courses, *RR*	72
XXVII.	To Each Her Own, *EM*	74
XXVIII.	Whale Call, *DHM*	76
XXIX.	Taking Shortcuts, *RR*	78
XXX.	Falling Off the Wagon Forever, *EM*	81
XXXI.	Underwater, *DHM*	83

❖ Autumn

	Doubt & Joy, *EM*	85
XXXII.	Mermaid 101, *DHM*	89
XXXIII.	Subterranean Adventures, *RR*	91
XXXIV.	Choices & Changes, *EM*	94
XXXV.	Dreams & Nightmares, *DHM*	96
XXXVI.	Rural Entertainment, *RR*	97
XXXVII.	The Sense of Time, *EM*	99
XXXVIII.	A Journey West, *DHM*	101
XXXIX.	Turkeys, *RR*	103
XL.	Talking Books, *EM*	105
XLI.	A Magical Samhain, *DHM*	107
XLII.	Comfort, *RR*	109
XLIII.	Hunting Words, *EM*	111
XLIV.	Wormholes & Slot Machines, *DHM*	113

❖ Winter

Winter Light, *EM*		115
XLV.	The Night the Animals Talk, *DHM*	116
XLVI.	Christmas Eve for the Family, *RR*	118
XLVII.	Cranking By Hand, *EM*	121
XLVIII.	Sassy, *DHM*	123
XLIX.	Appropriate Wrapping, *RR*	125
L.	Earth Secrets, *DHM*	128
LI.	Shoveling, *RR*	130
LII.	Wintergreen, *EM*	133
LIII.	Fondis Faeries, *DHM*	135
LIV.	Karen's List, *RR*	137
LV.	Winter Walk, *DHM*	142
LVI.	Epiphany, *RR*	144
LVII.	Rose, *DHM*	147
LVIII.	Faerie Cups, *EM*	149
LIX.	Imbolc, *DHM*	151
LX.	Love's Mistakes, *RR*	153

❖ Epilogue 157

PROLOGUE

We were imprisoned by snow: three feet of it. So was the rest of the county. Raul answered the phone when I called.

Yes, the animals were fine; no, the electricity hadn't dimmed; the wood stove was being fed regularly; running water was to be had, and, best of all, it looked like there wouldn't be any school for the rest of the week! "By the way," he asked conversationally, "Where are you, Daddy?"

"The front office of *The High Plains Rider*, with Deirdre Moon and Epona Maris, and wondering how I got here," I replied quietly, glancing at the two other couches on which my colleagues slept.

"Oh," he answered. "Well, have fun!" In the manner of those whose grasp of detail is not profound, he rang off, and I was left with a buzzing telephone receiver, still wondering.

The Womyn's Centre Fundraiser the night before had filled the 1,500-seat Fondis Lyceum. They'd come to hear Moon and Maris play, but they also were no less enthusiastic about the Celtic Crone Celebration or the Tibetan Barbershop Quartet. They'd even applauded me—although all I was doing was reading aloud.

I shook my head, remembering being seated in a folding chair backstage after our three encores. I must've fallen asleep. But why were the three of us in a place nearly two miles from there--six hours later?

"The faeries brought us," Deirdre said. She moved to a lotus position on the couch and looked directly at me as if she'd done so all her life. "They want us to spend some time together here."

I nodded, trying to think of a suitable experience I'd had that would have prepared me. I once believed I had a calling for the ministry, but reading the King James Bible had removed that.

"They left us well-stocked," she continued, looking at the wall behind me. "There's stuff left over from the Midwinter Party in the refrigerator; coffee and tea and drinks; all still good and needing to be consumed."

Epona stretched and opened her eyes. "You were right, Deirdre; the Bijou and West Ridge Ley lines do intersect here at the office. How pleasant!"

"Destiny's a funny thing," Deirdre said, "but it's something I have such faith in that I never question it. Mr. Rural, would you mind making a cuppa tea for me and a mug of coffee for Epona? You've been here the longest of the three of us and probably know your way around the kitchen better than we do. I know you like to keep busy when working on a new idea, and I imagine you'll find plenty of opportunities cooking for us."

I made the tea and coffee and pondered what she'd said. Of course, I'd known these two colleagues: I recommended each for the paper; but this was a side of them I'd never seen before.

"Last Beltane," Epona began, "I had a dream of three feathers drifting together in the wind that combs the ridgetop. One feather was from a crow, another from a hummingbird while the third came from a turkey's wing. I knew that the three of us would be writing something together, and I told my dream to Deirdre, who said, 'let's make it happen.' That's why we've sung and recorded together. Since you're formal and reserved, it took more time to bring you in; but we knew you'd be at the fundraiser last night, because it's the one charitable event you go to every year."

"And I merely provided the venue," Deirdre said. "The faeries concluded that the three of us should write a book together. While you would not be against such a project had we approached you formally, we really couldn't think of a time or a place where you wouldn't be distracted with ten thousand other projects."

I thought of my woodpile; the goats; the chickens roosting in the snow: they were right: I'd be distracted.

"Here, you cannot be distracted, Roger," she continued. "So, until the snow is passable, the three of us are to create a book called *The Fondis Chronicles.*"

"Why?" I asked.

"Destiny has some strange reasons," she answered, "but I prefer to look at the stars and realize that the moon and planets are singularly aligned to create something perfect."

"We have all the necessary materials," Epona observed, "and the room to create magic with them."

"And the three of us are going to live in a newspaper office and write essays or stories while the biggest news story to hit the county is sitting outside?" I asked in a bit of disbelief. "That snow must have wiped out whole herds of cattle; pipes must be frozen up and down the county—this needs to be covered!"

"That's what the telephone's for, Roger," Deirdre said gently. "It will soon ring with stories, which you will take down. You will also download their digital photos on the computer. The entire newspaper for this month will cover five days of hardship, which you can write about while contributing to *The Fondis Chronicles*."

She was right. The storm was covered in its entirety by me, sitting at a computer in the front office of *The High Plains Rider*. In addition, I managed to win a couple of Journalism awards, and perfected a way of cooking salmon and rice that was superb.

The snow was cleared five days after the New Year's Storm.

- Roger Rural

At the time, I believed Mr. Rural tended toward exaggeration. Now I am certain of it. Three feet of snow is *not* an imprisonment. If one considers the long term patterns of the weather gods, it is quite a cyclical event. The Snow Beings, in colleague with the Fondis Faeries of Flight, did manage to transport us in a most unusual fashion.

If you think it reverse sexism that I should have asked Roger Rural to do the kitchen duties, perhaps you are correct. I really needed to realign my aura after being whisked through time and space. If I were more evolved, I perhaps wouldn't have felt disoriented and needing a cellular restructuring. I'm not at all sure that Mr. Rural was on the same page with me.

The faeries twittered at that, knowing that literally we would be. Here. Now.

If you wonder how a dry witted, investigative reporter/farmer who once considered the ministry could get on with a walk-in from Sirius presenting as a representative of the Goddess, and a poet/horse whisperer who talks to geese, please proceed, gentle reader. It's an odd and intriguing trio, we three.

-Deirdre H. Moon

Odd, intriguing and generally fun to read, as you shall see if you have not given up on this enterprise before venturing forth into the unknown. Or "that which seems to be known, but perhaps isn't," to be more precise. If precision is of value to you, you may find some aspect of that here. Or perhaps not. The choice is yours, of course.

The salmon with rice was excellent.

-Epona Maris

Spring

TO BEGIN

Epona Maris

In order to begin, I must end.
The obvious endings, of course,
Like broken eggshells, cracked seed coats,
Shattered innocence.
The past grows inflexible as it hardens
Into nostalgic memories.
Prior decisions that each generation must endure
Until young wings grow strong enough
To force change.

In order to begin, I must end.
Stop procrastinating, stop worrying,
Stop all the preliminary practices of doubt
And just start.
But where? I stop again,
Hovering in tight spirals
Until wind currents blow my plans into sifting dust.

In order to understand, I must stop looking for answers
And open my eyes, instead,
To the world as it is
Or may be
If I allow my belief.
Look forward without expectations,
Open to peripheral visions mysterious
And profound
As the uncurling leaf of Spring.
Life reveals itself through chance moments,
Fleeting glances
And choices not followed.

In order to begin, I begin.
Let the chances flow where they may.

I.

SPRING WEDDING

Deirdre H. Moon

I stretch out my feet at a small, round wooden table on the porch of the Fondis Tea Room, sipping chai and people watching, neglecting my weathered copy of *Leaves of Grass*.

It is a brilliant April day with green bursting forth at every opportunity. Mellow strains of a fiddle drift across the street from the hotel as Bodini shifts from a blue grass warm up to that classic attributed to Henry VIII: "Greensleeves."

I smile and nod at the graceful woman in a sari as she walks down the street with her elegant afghan hound.

Fondis, long known for its diversity, is one of my favorite spots to visit artists and friends.

I'd hopped on my trusty mountain bike with a rainbow sheen, tooled down the narrow path from my yurt, concealed among the pines on the ledge above the Bijou. I usually have to drive the long way around to Fondis but today is Colorado brilliant. Lugh's blast of warming rays urge me from winter sloth.

Now, seated on the east side of the street, I turn as someone speaks my name. "Mr. Rural." I smile as he sidles into the chair next to me.

"Roger, please." I nod. "What brings you to town?" he asks.

"The wedding. And you?"

"Same. I've known Leslie and Saundra for years." Of course he would.

"Me too." I've only met Roger Rural a few times but read his commentaries on a regular basis.

"Actually, I'm officiating."

I didn't know that.

Clifford and Ronald, hand in hand, pause. "Hi, Deirdre," they say in unison, glance at each other, laugh. I introduce Roger.

"Are you going to Angel Fire and Luna's wedding?"

I nod.

Roger, always formal when first we meet, doesn't use the idiom of the day, but uses their formal names. He's very erudite even with his manners. I wouldn't say formal, just proper. And then his statements can really zing if you read between the lines. I wonder if he'll call Leslie "Angel Fire" and Saundra, "Luna" during the ceremony. I doubt it.

I look down the street, see the tall silhouette of the Ridge Writer as he ambles toward the tea house. It is rare to find these two witty guys in the same place at the same time. Usually they're crammed in black and white and read all over. Both of them urge one to open the mind and explore the possibilities.

Epona Maris, obviously one of my soul sisters, sits regally astride a sand colored Arabian steed who trots down Main Street.

They stop in front of me. Epona slips down from his great height. I look up to her great height. She straightens her earth tone garments with Celtic trim. I note her elaborate amber necklace. She tethers the beast and we hug.

By mid afternoon an eclectic, colorful group of townspeople, artists and out of towners wind their way along a path down to the stone circle by the river. The brides, dressed in tie-dyed silk gowns and matching floral coronations, glide sweetly through the crowd, greeting, hugging, kissing. Drums call in the earth energies.

I unwrap my bundle, spread a soft tartan blanket on the ground at the south of the Wheel, and settle, sliding my fingers into castanets, I add to the beat of the drums.

Belly to belly, then back to back, the Lady of the Lake and She Who Knows All begin to walk the circle in opposite directions. The Lady sprinkles rose petals and marigold blossoms. Knows All casts salt.

Cerridwen moves to the center of the circle, leaning heavily on her dragon tipped silver staff. She presides over the ceremony, a down to earth commitment between two women who love each other. The melodious tones of a flute linger in the air. Roger does the official, formal stuff, uniting the old ways with the new.

Musical instruments as varied as the people break forth in improvisational joy.

I'm always glad to linger in the company of good friends celebrating, especially in downtown Fondis as the full moon rises her smiling face of blessings on the gift of love between two people.

II.

THE LAW OF UNINTENDED CONSEQUENCES

Epona Maris

Discussions about the Law of Unintended Consequences are better conducted in a coffeehouse than in a bar, I decided, after comparing my notes from both settings. I had been back in Fondis for six months, this time, when I had the opportunity to complete that experiment.

I have been a cyclical resident of Fondis for years, returning when I need rest and inspiration, then setting off for the "real world" again to try my newly refurbished wings. I am a poet by trade, which gives me license for such vagaries as well as the time for contemplation. When I am "working" in that outside world, I spend my time on the lecture circuit, balancing budgets or signing books.

But when I'm in Fondis I spend much of my time riding other people's horses through the moonlit dark or engaging in philosophical discussions with miscellaneous locals. My inspiration comes from odd juxtapositions.

On the first occasion relevant to this subject, I was enjoying the simple pleasure of plain black coffee while seated by the fireplace in Carla's Coffeehouse. I watched the spring rain slick the sidewalks of Main Street in Fondis while Jimmy explained why his second trip through DUI classes would be more successful than the first.

"Last time I didn't think I needed it, but I was wrong. This time I'm paying attention." I thought back to the last time, two years ago, remembering how he white-knuckled his way through his mandated sobriety at the coffeehouse, then drifted across the street to the Fondis Bar as soon as his probation ended. "I can handle it," he said at the time, "and besides, all my friends are there."

I have been known to have a good time at the bar myself, so I knew a few things about Jimmy's friends there. Besides, as his cousin, I knew him well. He would have been better off changing his definition of the term "friends" and applying it to his non-drinking companions at the coffeehouse instead. But I didn't have to mention that to Jimmy now, since the county's finest had made the point quite well on the night he celebrated his promotion at work by buying rounds for the house until the house poured him out. Too much liquid makes it hard to hang onto the steering wheel on our bumpy dirt backroads.

Jimmy was now learning the virtues of black coffee for its own merits, rather than as a tonic for alcohol poisoning. Since I had taken my turn as a substance abuse counselor in a former life, I was pleased with myself for convincing him of that important distinction. "So what did you learn in last night's class?" I asked.

"You don't have to be drunk to be impaired," he answered. "Even two drinks can be too much." He smiled with the glow of the recent convert. "And there are a lot of people driving around without knowing they're impaired!"

I pondered the philosophical implications of that statement while Carla poured more coffee, her long black braid sliding past her shoulder.

"Some of those impaired people get away with things the rest of us have to pay for," she said with more heat than the coffee she poured. "Before I bought this coffeehouse, I worked in a bigger town in the front range," she explained. "The mayor used to stop in for coffee, but I would see him adding whisky from a flask. Sometimes the local cops had to drive him home, but sometimes they just followed him in case he went into a ditch. It saved them from having to take his car home for him to drive to work the next morning. And he always looked down on the guys at the bar. Just because you're elected to something, it doesn't mean you should be allowed to drive drunk."

Jimmy nodded his head. "The cops don't do that for guys like me, who work for a living."

"Of course, after the mayor drove his car onto the courthouse lawn, the people decided to vote him out." Carla set the coffee pot down with a satisfied thump.

"When I was a kid, I used to think that it was part of a sheriff's job description to drink," I said. "The county probably never had a sober sheriff until the residents decided that might be an occupational hazard."

Carla laughed. "What did they do then?"

"Voted in someone who promised not to drink. Of course, he did a few other things he should have promised not to do, like spend taxpayer money on a fleet of fancy new patrol cars when the budget wouldn't pay for enough deputies to drive them."

Jimmy looked into the coffee cup cradled between his big hands. "Sometimes it's hard to figure out what's the right thing to do." he said. I knew he was talking about more than politics.

I looked out the window in time to see a few rays of sunlight touching rainbow glints from the puddles in the street. Deirdre Moon chose that moment to stride purposefully down the sidewalk and the light sparkled on the crystals tied with magpie feathers in her hair. Her hair was mahogany dark this time, I noticed, which looked dramatic against the bright zig-zag pattern of her wool poncho. She looked like a woman on a mission, but she usually looks that way, even when waiting for friends to show up for tea. As she passed the window, a spotted rabbit tucked in the crook of her arm turned its head to glance at me before they vanished.

"Knowing what to do isn't the point," I said, inspired. "The point is to develop an awareness of unintended consequences." Jimmy and Carla just looked blankly at me.

"Every consequence you intend comes paired with one not intended," I explained. "Sometimes that can be a pleasant surprise but, more often than not, you won't like it much. The secret is to determine what that unintended consequence will be before you act. Otherwise it bites you someplace that hurts."

Jimmy nodded slowly. "At least thinking about that could slow you down before you do something dumb."

When I tried that argument at the bar, the next evening, most of Jimmy's friends were just confused.

III.

ADVENTURES IN CHICKEN-RAISING

Roger Rural

CHICKEN: *(n) 1. What your friends call you when you are reluctant to swim naked in a pool full of Jell-O; 2. A slang term for a female; 3. A domesticated descendant of the dinosaur.*

    There's a darn good reason the 4-H Poultry Book has a chart of "expenses" for its members to fill out, and a darn good reason why a parent's signature is required: with poultry, one doesn't make money. As a matter of fact, if one were inclined to look at the debits and credits column of my son's poultry raising schemes for the past three years, one would see that his father has burdened himself by almost $150.00. Net take over the same three years has totaled maybe $56.00.
    There's not much profit to poultry. Yet, some continually try to beat the odds, maybe because they're idealistic or stubborn or maybe just a little bit cursed.

    There's a sign down the road from me; at least, I think it's still there:
    1 Dz. Eggs Tow Dolors
    but it might be gone now, given the fact that the current homeowner doesn't have time to raise 1 dz. Eggs, let alone 2 dz, and it's kind of a shame because it marked the beginning and end of Chi's Poultry Empire: in dreams, though not practice, set to rival ConAGRA or Monsanto.
    Sherwood Anderson observed that most philosophers must have been raised on chicken farms, and he was probably correct, because just about every hopeful poultry experiment that's ever been winds up tanking.
    Chi was a mail order bride from someplace "back east:" a bit farther east than New York; and when Marc, a guy who fixed big trucks, married her, chickens were not in their futures. The English language certainly wasn't, either, given his taciturnity and her inability to communicate. How they handled daily affairs was certainly interesting as well: Their shopping was performed by one of those food service delivery companies that stocked the freezer once a month

and Marc took care of the chores and probably paid the bills. He would leave each morning and she would clean house, prepare meals, and, I think, try to learn English from the television and the radio.

And I would have never known of her existence if it had not been for a chicken, which surprised me as much as I surprised it when it suddenly appeared at my southern fence line, and endeavoring to escape, jammed its head between the wires of my fence.

Chi showed up a few seconds later, out of breath, and smiling at me, pointed to the chicken. Clearly, she wanted that chicken; so I bent the wire a bit with my pliers, grabbed the chicken by its feet so it was carried upside down, and walked up to Chi. Chi nodded and started walking back to her house. Clearly, I was supposed to follow.

One of the most ridiculous sights to my mind is a chicken being carried by its legs. Its little head is still looking around as if in flight, keenly assessing its surroundings while its wings uselessly flap backwards, kind of like a mischievous kid going to the principal's office.

After crossing the majority of the four acres where she lived, Chi beckoned me to a door at the side of her barn, which she cautiously opened. I just as cautiously followed, leaving the door open behind me.

The barn, which had originally been designed to house a couple of horses and maybe a truck, had shelves built about every two feet along its interior, lining every wall, going up to six feet, so there were three tiers. I recognized them immediately as roosts, capable of holding probably 500 chickens, if not more.

Chi beckoned me to the far end of the barn, where she had a long shallow water trough on the floor and a feeder big as a train boiler and as tall as she was. Its opening spilled scratch grains that some messy poultry had scattered. Nearby, on one of the shelves, roosted six chickens of various breeds. Chi took the chicken which I still carried, cradled it a moment, then set it next to its brethren.

Clearly proud of what she was doing, she took me to the old tack room of the barn, where an incubation unit sat and pens stood ready to keep chicks warm.

A Murray Mac Murray poultry catalogue sat on the floor by the incubator, well worn and well thumbed.

Clearly, this woman was going to raise chickens in a big way: "In spring. In spring" she kept saying, pointing to the catalogue almost frenetically.

And did she? In late March, boxes and boxes of chicks, tiny balls of fluff, arrived, were promptly put into the warming pens, kept there for a month, given the "crumbles" of nutrients that they needed, then were released to the barn, to join the rest of the flocks, where they'd be put into their "pecking order" and then go lay eggs.

At least that was what happened at the beginning. In April, a stray dog got into the barn and killed about half the flock; in September, an early frost froze the water and killed some more.

And eggs: Chi could never find very many customers for them. She wound up with a whole refrigerator full.

They left abruptly early the next year. Marc found employment elsewhere and Chi, with only one quarter of her flock remaining, about thirty chickens, drowned them in that long trough and left their bodies in the barn, surrounded by all those empty shelves.

But I wasn't to know that, then.

"Your name?" she asked.

"Roger."

"Who?"

"Roger."

"Oh."

"That's fine," I assured her. "Your name?"

She seemed to sneeze.

"That's fine, Chi," I said.

She nodded. "O? I can call you?" She indicated her empty shelves, awaiting the poultry.

"Yes," I assured her, grabbling the Murray Mac Murray Catalogue, scribbling my name and number on it.

And the only call I ever got was from her husband, Marc, who thanked me for helping rescue the chicken. "It meant a lot to her," he volunteered, "because she's got dreams."

IV.

EXERCISE INTERRUPTUS

Deirdre H. Moon

Sassy and I walked briskly along the path around Lake Fondis. I needed the escalated heart rate so I joined Sassy, hoping to engage her latent spiritual interests. It was probably hopeless. She wouldn't even align her chakras before we started out.

New green grass brightened the horizon. Tulips, crocus and hyacinths bobbed in garden borders along the jogging trail.

My cell phone dipsy-doodled out its melodious cacophony. I shrugged a shoulder at Sassy and answered.

"Wildflower Earthwater? No way!" Now I shrugged both shoulders and raised an eyebrow. Sassy wasn't looking.

Wildflower is my cousin, daughter of my father's sister. I haven't seen her in years. Last time we hung out was at a theatre commune in Maine. She struck out to make it big in Hollywood. I stayed and did the New England little theatre circuit.

"Wildflower, where are you?" The classic cell phone query.

Sassy was hoofing it on ahead of me. Oh well. I slowed, walked over to the little dock where the Lake Keeper kept his rowboat, certain he wouldn't mind if I dangled my feet. It was a balmy April day.

I'd seen Wildflower a few times on TV: commercials, bit parts, talk shows. If you haven't heard of her, don't worry. She never made it big. Had a SAG card but not much else. Her fifteen minutes of fame blew quietly away in a Santa Monica breeze. I'd wondered where she was, just never googled her to find out.

"Fondis International Airport? I can't wait to see you." Did I lie? Wildflower is such a flake. Some people think I am. Wait 'til they meet my cousin. I'm mainstreaming it by comparison. I like her but she's just too over the edge. And now she was here. In *my* town.

She tried to ditch her wild ways, merge with the corporate world; worked as a stockbroker for a while and knew the market before anyone could spin it up or down.

But she invested in green stocks that didn't do much. When a new manager came in, she was canned. He didn't like her nose ring, tattoo or attitude.

"I'll be there as soon as I can." I rang off, glancing ahead. Sassy was a bobbing spec in the distance.

"Sassy," I spoke to my cell phone, voice activating her number on the auto dial.

"Hi, Sass. That was my cousin Wildflower Madrona Earthwater. She just flew into Fondis International. I'm going to pick her up."

"Deirdre, I'll back track and take you." Sassy was so helpful. I wondered if her car was running these days.

"No problem. Keep jogging for both of us. Besides she'll like Edgar." I punched off, clipped the cell on my waist band and headed back.

"Edgar, you'll have to carry some suitcases home." Edgar Rice Burro nickered and continued to munch grass where he was tethered at the trail head.

V.

IN AND AMONG GROWING THINGS

Roger Rural

Above the leeching field, the vegetables grow:
Pumpkins, squash, peppers, onions, row on row.
Potatoes, corn, spinach, broccoli, turnip greens,
And if they aren't ravaged, several varieties of beans.
*(with apologies to John McRae, who wrote
"In Flanders Fields")*

Growing Things: *(compound noun; collective noun):1. Any species of thistle, weed, or obnoxia that one tries to eradicate with good garden practices; 2. Pertaining to something that stacks cell on cell, rather like a honeycombed penitentiary; 3. How one excuses an adolescent's insatiable hunger for Pop Tarts instead of salad.*

When Mrs. Rural and I occupied a house in the city, our first landscaping project involved turning a scraggly patch of grass, measuring 15' x 15', into a garden.

"Anyone can garden," she told me, "even you."

My idea of gardening at the time was limited to occasional fertilizing, occasional watering, and occasional mowing of a tufted batch of grass whimsically called a lawn.

"Take the shovel like this," she said. "Dig deep. Turn the earth: it can take it and it enjoys the sunlight. Break up the clods—yeah, like that—so everything's ready for seeds. You'll be surprised at what we accomplish."

We were both rather young, then, and often were distracted from our garden by college and career plans and all those incredible fits and starts of early adulthood that require so much energy but really mean nothing, like texturing a ceiling for no reason, other than to say that we could do it; or holding a party for my cousin and his latest girlfriend.

"We'll plant some tomatoes over there," Mrs. Rural indicated, "and try some beans on this side, and put potatoes here—" Her voice faded off.

"Kind of ambitious, isn't it? Let's start with some tomatoes."

So we did. We watered them when we thought about it; remarked about how green they were at first, and seemed never to have the time to plant anything else in that first garden. After all, we were distracted with many other things.

We harvested sixteen tomatoes that summer and a ton of weeds: all attracted by the fresh earth we'd turned.

"It's a start, isn't it?" she asked cheerfully. "Maybe next year, we'll grow more."

I was inclined to agree. After all, it was the first time I'd ever committed myself to growing things.

Our second or third garden was a lot more organized. We had tomatoes, beans, and onions: all in specific sections—far apart from one another, but close enough to make weeding easy. Turning the earth that spring had actually been fun because I was no longer being shown; I was an equal partner in the endeavor. The harvest was small, but it was another hopeful sign that we'd do better the next year.

We'd stopped some of our more time-consuming distractions by then: textured ceilings no longer had the same fascination and parties for our swinging relatives became passe'.

"Keep working on it," the experts told us. "You'll watch the garden grow healthy and strong. Don't give up if it's a little messy or sometimes it needs weeding or grass gets on the borders. Gardens are that way."

Dick Ehrlich and his wife, Charlotte, have probably been gardening since the Spanish-American War on land just south of Fondis, and regularly compare notes with Miss Sadie Smith, a neighbor on five acres up the hill from them, who's also been gardening since the McKinley Administration. Sadie grows the biggest, firmest, and finest pumpkins in the county. "I don't let a weed or blade of grass grow in my garden," she declares firmly. "If I see one, I pounce on it."

"Fine pumpkins," Dick has observed to me, "but it'd be hell to be one in her garden. Rather have a few weeds and blades of grass, even if it means a smaller pumpkin."

"You don't really know much about the actual growing, do you?" Mrs. Rural asked me by the time our fourth or fifth garden was being planned. We'd moved to the suburbs that year and had bought a house where nothing had grown for a long time except beer cans and cigarette butts. "So—why don't you do something else?" she asked.

"Something that is part of the whole garden but not part of the growing things?"

We hit upon the idea of a raised bed—a planter, really, measuring 10' x 15', standing three feet high and made of redwood 2x6 planks, filled with compost, manure, and soil—all of which I would build and provide. "Let's make something permanent," she said, "that everybody knows is our garden. Nobody can touch it with a lawnmower or a shovel to remove it." Around it grew a patio and flowers in small barrels. It flourished during the five years we lived there.

When Charlie was married to Christine, she made a small garden in their front yard and kept it composted and healthy, full of the herbs she cooked with, weed-free, until her sister and two children moved into the house. Then the garden wasn't as important. It was taken over by weeds. A landscaping company Charlie hired killed the weeds and replanted grass. It lies as a depression in the soil now.

We have had various gardens over the years: each an improvement over its predecessor. I am no longer expected to help in the planting, except to turn the earth. I build and maintain the fence around the garden. I also carry compost, lay down black plastic between the rows of beans and tomatoes, and water. Mrs. Rural and the children plant and harvest.

We have had a fine crop of potatoes and squash this year with a few onions and carrots. The tomatoes, planted too late, withered on the vine. Maybe we'll plant them on time next year.

Grass and weeds grow on our borders and sometimes between our plants. They are pulled and tossed into the field around the garden, where they can grow however they will—like the study of textured ceilings or parties for swinging relatives: those things don't interest us much anymore.

We have been gardening for twenty years.

VI.

HISTORY WHERE YOU LEAST EXPECT IT

Deirdre H. Moon

"Oh my goddess," Lilith groaned and pressed back into the cushioned booth at the Fondis AM, my favorite breakfast place.

"What?" I asked leaning forward so she could whisper her distress across the table.

"Don't look now. It's Liddy Paca and that Celtic French woman what's her name?" She slid deeper into her seat. "Master gardeners."

I looked. Curiosity is my bane.

After all, we were here to look and it was all her idea. The Fondis AM is a restaurant/radio station combo. The polished hardwood floors lead right up to the glass fronted sound booth at the back of the restaurant where you can check out the most liberal of Fondis thinkers up close and personal—plus catch a few tunes. Lilith had a crush on the morning DJ, Rip Roar.

Even while she had her eye on Rip, she'd seen Liddy and the Highland Lass as they passed the window.

"Deirdre," they said in unison, pointing from the entrance. I waved and they worked their way through the crowd to our booth.

"May we join you?" Liddy asked as she scooted in next to Lilith, who frowned.

"I was just leaving for the women's room." Lilith pushed against Liddy's arm and they both slid out.

The Highland Lass gave me a hug after she plopped books and papers on the table.

"What are you two up to?" I asked, paying more attention to my dangling preposition than to Lilith's abrupt departure.

"Oh, just wait 'til you see these," the Highland Lass enthused and rummaged in her satchel.

"We're back in Master Gardening classes," Liddy Paca explained.

The Lass was rifling through a stack of 8 x 10 photos. "Look at this."

I looked at a weird tight shot of some 1950s monster movie demon.

"Gotcha, huh? A thrip magnified 450 times. Cool, eh?" She had stacks of them, bugs and pollen and nasty things that became fascinating under a high powered lens.

"Let me tell you about ergots on rye," Liddy Paca said.

"Do I want to know? It doesn't sound good for breakfast." I pushed my carrot cake aside, ready to be enlightened.

"No photos of those, sorry," the Lass lamented.

"Ergots are the fruiting structure of the fungus that grows on rye."

"Rye was the grain of the masses throughout much of history. When rye went awry, things got crazy," the Lass chuckled at her own joke.

"Crazy like St. Anthony's Fire," Liddy Paca explained.

"In exceedingly cool and moist conditions, the ergot fungus thrived. When people ate the bread, they often suffered from St. Anthony's Fire causing hallucinations, miscarriages, burning in the limbs, gangrene and most often death."

"I knew this wasn't a breakfast subject." I sipped some chai.

"St. Anthony's Fire really reduced the population in Europe. Then it hit here and we see the Salem Witchcraft Trials. Those people weren't possessed, they were suffering from fungal infection."

"Wow."

"Contains the same active ingredient as LSD."

"Double wow. I think Lilith is right."

"About?"

"Master Gardeners are scary." We all laughed. They bundled up their educational paraphernalia and headed back toward the sound booth. Rip Roar was going to interview them.

Lilith passed them with a nod and sat down. "Did you hear that?"

"Nope but what I heard was historical."

"I was just on the radio with Rip Roar and you didn't hear it? He asked me out. Right there on the air. With all of Fondis listening. Can you believe it?"

There were a lot of beliefs to consider today. I nodded and smiled. She was blissed.

VII.

A FLOW OF WORDS

Epona Maris

When are words in season? There are seasons for planting and for sowing, for hunting deer or wild turkeys. We say that asparagus is in season when the price is cheap and snow is out of season when we get flurries along the ridge in June. There is a time to be born and a time to die; there is certainly a season for grieving.

I thought that words would flow for me once I had everything set up just right: I had finished college and returned home in time to ease my father's dying days. My mother and I grew closer during that time, so I felt comfortable that we had said all of the right things to each other by the time she too passed, a few months later. I was on my own, with no shelter between me and my own mortality, but my grieving had been done in the days before their deaths. Or so I felt at the time.

I inherited the house but felt no strong attachment to it. I thought once it sold, I would move someplace exotic, but something kept drawing me back to Fondis. I built a small log cabin among the trees on the ridge. I had a view of the mountains, a little stream in the backyard, and acres of space to myself. It was the start of my career as a poet and I had the perfect environment to write. I was ready, but the words were not.

My mother had died in the fall, in late October, season of the dying year, long nights of chilly introspection. I had passed through the winter alone and the daffodils were shouting springtime, season of growth and rebirth, time for all things to bloom into fruition. I sat at my table by the window and watched the world flush with green. I felt the empty space within me where seeds of words had always sprouted, ripe for the waiting page. The page remained a fallow field.

I took to walking the hills, wandering among trees, too restless to sit alone with my emptiness. The trees whispered to me, but I couldn't understand them. At times I would catch a sight of those who live between the worlds, but I couldn't hear the words of wisdom they might have shared with me. The faerie folk offered suggestions that were entertaining to perform, but produced no poetry. The people in town were dull and uninspiring.

The season was flowing into true spring when I met Deirdre Moon on a forest trail one morning, wrapping her skirts about her knees so they wouldn't catch in the bicycle spokes. Lost in my own thoughts, I almost passed her by with just the courteous greeting one shares with acquaintances one bumps into on the street, but my feet stopped of their own accord. "I don't have words," I blurted out, then felt really dumb.

"You have them," she said, "but you're not living them." After settling her hat, she pedaled slowly down the trail. I turned to watch her go, not sure if I should say thank you.

That evening, I took pen and paper to the field behind my parent's home, the place where I grew up, the home of my memories. As strangers turned on the lights, I could almost see my parents through the shining windows. "I miss you," I told them, for the first time since they were gone. The words flowed.

VIII.

SPORT

Roger Rural

Sport *(n)* 1. *An athletic activity;* 2. *To display, as in "You are sporting new ostrich feathers, Irma;"* 3. *To make fun of, as in "He was being made sport of by his colleagues;"* 4. *A slurred commendation of a sweet after-dinner liquor, as in "Dis Port is really gud."*

    Lydia and Marie, both fourteen, whisper and giggle over the phone together, sometimes for hours at a time. It's a form of sport among the less interesting human beings, called gossip, usually.
    "Helen really did that?" Lydia asks incredulously, then giggles, already knowing the answer.
    "Yes!" Marie replies, enjoying the deliciousness of it all: the delirious knowledge of their pugnacious classmate, Helen, who indiscreetly told Marie about her activities with a boy she thought she loved.
    Whatever it was that Helen did was news for the entire softball team at practice the next day: Lydia and Marie made sure of it. And Helen endured the giggles and remarks while she practiced her pitching. She was good at pitching: as accurate as any boy, and sometimes better with a fastball. Marie was up to bat.

Soccer, for five year-olds, is a curious sport;
Played, by twenty of them, on a basketball court.
The ball careens around the poor patient coach,
And the children bash into him without reproach.

I paid forty-five dollars to watch my daughter run around,
To scrape her knees on the floor, then run aground
And tell me she's tired as the opposite team scores:
Seven to zero, and there's about forty more.

    Sport builds character, I think. I encourage my daughter to be aggressive and to kick the ball. Injuries to her teammates and to the opposite team are to be ignored. That's not very sporting, really. *It is not the character that I strive for.*

Striving in sport is something Chris knows all about. When he played baseball and football, he was considered weak because of his small frame and flailing arms. But he developed them into a well-coordinated machine by the time he was a sophomore in high school. That's what made him such a valuable lieutenant in the fire department: he would build the firefighters the same way he'd built himself: into a cohesive unit of awesome potential.

But the problem, right now, is that he and five of his best firefighters lost the Barrel contest at the Fondis Fourth. A barrel is stretched along a cable fifteen feet above Mainstreet and groups of firefighters have a go with a pressurized hose, trying to move it from one side to the other. Chris and his team had lost to a bunch of guys from Charlie's Bar last July.

So Chris hired a couple of fellas to place posts and put up a fifteen-foot high cable behind Station One. He bought a barrel from Fondis Liquor and mounted it. In the training he supervises on Saturday afternoons, Chris makes sure every firefighter is able to move that barrel with the hose pressure. He and his department won't ever be subjects of sport about this again.

Mortimer Evans III is one of those kids anyone would instantly feel sorry for. At age 14, pimply and gawky; too tall for his movements, he's lost: bumping into trashcans, saying "S'cuse me," to doors that bang his bottom: a weapon of mass destruction without realizing it. But he's good in school. He was leading the pack in Math and Science last year; and his English grades weren't too shabby, either. Probably because he didn't have many friends, he could settle down and study on those long Saturday nights when his classmates were wasting time at Rip N Run and other emporia.

A kid like this is naturally drawn to taking care of animals, if such a thing is available to him, because he finds a basic need met in feeding and knowing the animal. That's why Morty had a sheep and a goat at the County Fair. He'd even gone beyond that: he'd built a wooden cornsheller for display and included all the designs for it, painstakingly rendered from books he'd studied, then mounted in the Agricultural Building for public display.

He'd hoped his friend, Brandon, newly-moved to Fondis, would appreciate what he'd done; and invited Brandon to see it. Brandon was the closest thing Morty had to a friend: they'd dissected a tapeworm together last year and they'd written a short story for English about a girl who was misunderstood.

"Of course we can pick him up, Morty," his mother assured him when the topic was broached. "You know I like for you to have friends." And Morty wished his mother was the young and glamorous woman his father had fallen in love with; not the grey-haired driver of the ten year-old Buick that smelled of cats.

"Have a nice time, boys," she said as she dropped them off.

"Bye, Mom," Morty intoned

Brandon was from Los Angeles. He'd mentioned that to Morty before and he wondered why Morty wasn't impressed. In Los Angeles, they did not have goats or sheep and they could have cared less about a cornsheller. Morty knew it would be a long afternoon. Brandon was too hot; Brandon was too tired; Brandon was too bored.

"Mom—"Morty tentatively asked, "We aren't like the folks in Los Angeles, are we?"

"No, I don't suppose we are," she replied.

The ball hit Edith in the face with the vengeance of 100 miles per hour and broke her nose. What a shame, Helen thought. Edith wouldn't be making sport for awhile.

IX.

THE MISTRESS OF LOCH FONDIS

Deirdre H. Moon

"So, what's all this malarkey about water spirits," She Who Doubts asked. "Next thing ya know, you'll be telling me the Lock Ness Monster's real and his cousin is living in Fondis."

I laughed. "Well. A deep subject," I quipped. "All of them full of water spirits."

"What *are* you talking about?" She'd totally missed the old pun.

"Wells. Water spirits. You know." I knew she didn't. "I'll cut to the chase." She checked her watch. "Of course Nessie is real."

"Nessie?"

I sighed. "The Loch Ness Monster as you call her. It is a tragic misnomer to call her a monster. She's actually very sweet in her own way."

"Get out. How would you know?" She fidgeted, frowned, clicked an acrylic thumb nail against acrylic fingernail.

"The last time I was in Scotland I connected with the Loch Ness Monster as you refer to her. But the point is that there are many of her species in the world and..."

"Really, Deirdre, you slay me. Get a grip. There is not a Loch Ness Monster. There are no big feet except on basketball players. There are no..."

It was my turn to interrupt. "Let me tell you what happened at Beltane." I gave it an Irish pronunciation. "Okay. May Day. We all gathered in the Fondis Park around the May Pole." I grinned thinking of that phallic symbol, such an accepted icon in the park. "Kids and moms and dads and old folks, each grabbed a colorful ribbon and danced to the spontaneous music." True community spirit.

"Deirdre, dear, gotta run. Pedicure. You know. Catch ya later." She clicked her high heels off to her SUV and left me standing there with the best part of the story untold.

It happened at sunset as the central fire blazed high in the brick court yard on the west side of town, near the lake.

Cerridwen joined me with the Lady of the Lake and Barbarella. What had been a dust cloud settled as Epona rode in on her handsome steed. She slid off the horse with tai chi grace to walk with us from the park down to the lake. Geese flew overhead, blue birds darted for the forest.

Cerridwen began chanting an ancient incantation to the water spirits. We all joined her, settling on a grassy bank as the last glittering rays of sunshine silhouetted cattails.

"Look, Gran'ma, I never saw that rock before." Cerridwen's granddaughter Fiona pointed. The old woman struggled to her feet, leaning on her silver headed dragon staff . A smile glimmered at the creases of her mouth.

"There is no rock there, wee lassie. It's a visitor." By now we were all on our feet. Cerridwen motioned for us to be still and let out a long, low, primal moaning. I shivered. The sound was returned in kind as the long shiny neck of the creature emerged from the water.

"She's glad we're here," murmured Cerridwen.

"Who is it, Gran'ma?" the child asked, tugging her grandmother's skirts.

"The Mistress of Loch Fondis," she replied.

"Where's the key, Gran'ma?"

Cerridwen smiled. "Loch, not lock. She is the key." Cerridwen patted her granddaughter's shoulder. "Loch means lake, little one. She is the keeper of the lake. She wants us to know that she holds the portal open for the energies here, that we are to remember her when we dance, when we sing, when we speak to one another. There is magic here."

We stood in darkness holding hands, believing.

X.

THE PROBLEM WITH ACTION

Roger Rural

"Every public action which is not customary, either is wrong or, if it is right, is a dangerous precedent. It follows that nothing should ever be done for the first time."
--Francis MacDonald Cornford (1874-1943)

  In Ayn Rand's *Atlas Shrugged*, a certain type of electric railroad engine was always supposed to be parked near the foot of a mountain tunnel in order to aid the larger trains in a steep ascent. Once gaining the ascent, the engine was unhooked, rode down, and was parked again in anticipation of its next journey. Since it was electric, it spewed no asphyxiating fumes for passengers or crew to choke on in the tunnel. So—someone who believed that taking action immediately removed the electric locomotive and replaced it with a coal-burner. When the coal-burner was used to haul the next large train through the tunnel, the crew and passengers were all asphyxiated. This is the problem of action.

> "The best of all our actions tend
> To the preposterousest end."
> --Samuel Butler (1612-1680)

  But action, Sanders reflected, is not just in fiction. It's everywhere. His son, Alex, decided finally to propose to his fiancée. Both of them were going to be schoolteachers, and they liked each other well enough, and they both had the possibility of good jobs in Denver, far away from the farm near Fondis: closer to her parents. Her parents were pretty active: they spent winters in Las Vegas and their summers in the mountains, west of Denver. Her dad, an attorney, had made his money on insurance claims: prosecuting bogus ones, Sanders recalled, and the insurance companies were happy to pay him for his success. Andrea, Alex's fiancée, was accustomed to having a late model car, clothes that fit and were stylish, and accustomed to comfort. Sanders smiled at the memory of Alex's wonder, early on in their college romance: Her computer wouldn't download music fast enough; "so she went out and just bought another computer—just for music!"

That gave Sanders pause. That Alex was the boyfriend of a girl who could spend money like that! He looked at his old Ford pickup, parked next to the pig trailer: although it wasn't used often, when it was, it served well. The springs showed through in the seat in places, and the radio had long ago been torn out; but first gear was solid and powerful, and it would haul pigs and goats and cattle behind it. He couldn't see Andrea, his future daughter in law, ever using such a truck or even being in such a truck.

Action: We love the word. It bespeaks youth and effectiveness and GETTING SOMETHING DONE. It speaks of frustration with the status quo and a gnawing desire to change; no matter what the consequences.

A new County Commissioner who will "shake the courthouse" is voted in; and in trying to "shake" the establishment, finds that her rhetoric and her threats to "change" are meaningless because the folks in the Courthouse are already working at less-than-acceptable wages, and only do so because of a spirit of public service.

A new Principal is hired at the high school who will "move the comfortable faculty" finds that the "comfortable" faculty is really his best workforce because they are the ones who know how the political and social climate works: these are the lessons of Action.

Shortsighted action, or action for its own sake, is meaningless and detrimental. Although satisfying in the short run, it's disastrous in the long run.

The Founding Fathers were wise in framing The Constitution of the United States of America: they made it virtually impossible for those seeking action to immediately receive it. Ratification, for a Constitutional Amendment, is two-thirds of fifty states. They made sure of it for the same reason Sanders asked his son:

"Why do you want to marry her?"

"Because I love her."

"You gonna live on love?"

"No. We'll get regular pay."

"Can she live on regular pay?"

Alex thought about it. "No," he said simply and profoundly.

He'd always reminded his father of the guy on the Tarot deck who kept pulling on a plant in the hopes that it *would grow faster, and he'd graduated early from high school, took the minimum number of courses in college to get out as soon as possible, and seemed always on the go: a man of action who'd driven home to do his laundry and would then turn around and spend the rest of the evening in the University library doing research for a paper that he'd turn in early. Sanders briefly wondered if action wasn't a substitute for not facing his mother's death, which had happened when Alex was a senior in high school.*

"No. We'd have to supplement with her dad's money," Alex concluded.

Sanders pulled two beers from the fridge, set them on the table and opened them. He and his son hadn't shared a beer for awhile.

"But she wants to get married right away, Dad; and her mother has already told a bunch of people. What happens if I say no?"

Sanders considered. "I don't want you to do anything dishonorable," he said. "I only want my future daughter in law to know what sort of man she's marrying. She's going to spend the spring break with us: here, in Fondis."

"Dad; we've got plans—"Alex protested.

"—So do I," Sanders cut him off. "Tell her to pack her workshirts and jeans. I'll scrub down the spare room for her. And—"A sudden thought struck him—"I'll call her daddy to see if it's all right. What's the number?"

"Ed? Chris Sanders here. Uh huh. Alex's dad. Yeah. I'm fine. Say—in about two week's time, with the pigs farrowing and the lambing and the new chicks, I'm gonna need Alex's help and I wondered if Andrea couldn't spend that week out here, too. I know: they were thinking about Fort Lauderdale, but Alex can't afford that and I need him here. Yeah—Alex just cancelled his hotel and airfare. You know they charge twenty percent for a refund?

"Will you ask her if she'd like to come out? Thanks."

Sanders hung up the phone. If Andrea came out and tried to help, he figured, she'd be a good egg as a daughter in law. It wouldn't be just "action."

XI.

ANSWERS FROM A TREETOP

Deirdre H. Moon

Wildflower Earthwater eases gracefully out of a headstand, an exact mirror of my movements.

I'm annoyed. I tried doing yoga to escape her incessant need to process. So, she doesn't talk while I go through my asanas, she just follows along. Perfectly.

She's been here a month. Living with me in the yurt. A one person, one cat, one dog yurt. Two humans is too much.

Wildflower is my cousin, a person I share much in common with and whom I truly love. But a month? Good Goddess, it's been a long one.

Her energy zips around knocking into me when I least expect it. Oh, she's helpful. Too helpful, perhaps. I waken to the clatter of dishes as she scurries around the kitchen making breakfast before dawn. She's already fed the donkeys. I'm not a morning person.

She waters the plants and trims them back. I thought they were doing just fine.

Really, I must get a grip. She's healing from a sour love affair and won't be here long. I hope. Last week she brought a college student home, some dude ten plus years her junior. She's in high caretaker mode. I could tell she was going to ask him to spend the night and I said I could give him a ride back to town if he needed it. She walked him down the trail instead, returning hours later. Whatever.

I pull on my hiking boots, lace them up. She's doing the lunch dishes, singing old time rock 'n' roll with the radio. Maine coon kitty Merlin is rubbing her ankles. I grab a handful of carrots from the fridge.

"I'm going for a walk. Be back later," I say.

"Hang on. I'll go with you."

"I need to be alone."

"Whatever. Besides, I'm waiting for a phone call." She begins to rearrange the silverware drawer.

After offering carrot treats to the donkeys, I head up the cliff trail to the Meditation Tree, my favorite Ponderosa pine. The tree spirit always soothes me. I climb the perfectly spaced branches and settle at the top, my arms around the trunk. To the distant east I can see Kansas. Colorful orange and lavender clouds catch the late day sun. To the west, a lightning storm dances along the Rockies. I breathe the sky, feel the earth, release my angst to the Universe.

I'm in a much better mood when I get back to the yurt. Wildflower walks out of the bathroom.

"Wow, you look smashing." She does—all dressed up in a tight black mini-skirt and a clingy, low scooped, cleavage revealing tee. Eyeshadow, liner, blush and berry red lips. She grins.

"Can we talk? I have so much to tell you and I've needed to be more clear with you." No kidding. She slips off her sling back heels and sinks into the lotus position, flashing red panties. I follow suit, only I'm wearing leggings.

"Deirdre, you're the best cousin anyone could have and I'm so grateful for this time with you. I feel like I could stay here forever."

Goddess forbid. I zip my lip and listen. My turn will come.

"Well, that's not the point. I need more to do. It's kinda lonely up here. And I had a series of phone calls that just put it all together for me. Tomorrow I start a job at the library, part time. Second part time job will be tending bar at the Fondis Country Club. Should be good tips."

An answer to my prayers. My limited budget won't have to support two now.

"Your friend Raven who lives in the adobe on the cliffs needs a house sitter for six months and I'm moving over there this weekend."

Great Goddess, how quickly things can turn around. For all this, she's dressed like a model?

"And—this is the big news—and, Thunder Marin is coming to pick me up for our first date." She's grinning like the Cheshire cat.

"I thought you liked that kid that was here last week, what's his name?"

Wildflower laughed. "A diversion, only. Thunder and I have been talking whenever I'm in town." She's dreamy eyed. Thunder, rumored to be in line as the next fire chief, is dark eyed, curly haired, strong jawed handsome, built like a Bowflex ad. And single. Many Fondis women have lusted after him. I'm flabbergasted.

"Wow. I'm really happy for you, Wildflower."

"Me too. You're the best, Deirdre. Thanks for everything."

The chimes twinkle around the yurt, announcing her visitor. I stick a finger into the soil of an African violet. I'll water my own plants tonight. The faeries twitter around the circle of my dwelling. Things work out when you let them.

XII.

A TRUE BELIEVER

Roger Rural

Lawrence Kutch had seen at least eighty summers and was getting ready for his eighty-first that March. Calving would start soon enough, he knew, resulting in his spending most nights in the barn; but right now, in the early days of the month, he could still enjoy the warmth of the house, close to Ronnie. The weather still spit snow and the wind was bitter: Ronnie would have to wear a sweater again today over his shirt. "Which one'll it be, Ronnie?" Lawrence asked, yawning. "The red one? Why not?" And he dressed Ronnie in one of the many sweaters Evelyn had knitted and given him for Christmas years before. It hung loose on Ronnie, but Ronnie just grinned.

"*That old guy,*" *Diana mused, as their truck navigated past the Kutch house on Road Three, "has been living virtually alone in that house, keeping those cattle and harvesting alfalfa year after year. Why doesn't he just retire and move into town? Let someone else take over. Doesn't he have a couple of boys?*"

"With boys of their own," her husband, Ulises, answered. "Maybe he just doesn't know how to quit. Kind of like how he views the Party."

She laughed. "A true believer, he is. Voting Republican will bring the country back to the values and the selflessness that have made this country great," she intoned. "Don't you still believe that?"

"Yeah," he smiled, "But I'm a little more realistic about it. How'd I get to be County Party Chair if I weren't?"

She knew his argument: the more doctrinaire Republicans in the County believed in Party Victory at Any Price, and so supported some local candidates who were less than savory or honest. As Party Chair, it was Ulises' job to deliver the votes, which he did well. Folks like Lawrence, on the other hand, had pretty well left the Party because of that.

"All I know is if the Democrats put up a candidate with enough money and time—"

"Yeah, I know; I know," he replied, shifting the truck into fourth gear.

There were whole days when Lawrence didn't see or talk to anyone but Ronnie and the Herefords, which was just fine with him. Talking took work and had become increasingly unpleasant, especially if it concerned politics.

"I'll tell ya', Ronnie," he was saying as he measured two fingers of Bourbon, one for himself, and one for his companion, "They just don't understand that we were fighting for the country then. Defense was slashed and that Jimmy Carter was doing everything to make us a Third World Country! And now look at us! Second to none, and because they're successful and the County's voting a straight Republican ticket, we elect a bunch of nincompoops like that woman who gets in and changes all the zoning laws so businesses can build on a floodplain! What kind of sense is that!"

Ronnie just grinned, looking overly large because of the sweater Lawrence had dressed him in. Lawrence stirred the green beans as he began grilling the pork chops. "Won't drink your Bourbon?" he asked. He smiled back at Ronnie, then drank Ronnie's Bourbon himself.

In the meeting room of the Fondis County Republicans, there were scrapbooks dating back to the first year of the County's existence. Ulises took one down and idly leafed through it: 1976. There were photos of a coffee, it looked like, and posing with Lawrence and Evelyn was Ronald Reagan. There were a couple of other photos from the same gathering. 1977: a cocktail party. There was Ronald Reagan again. 1978: same. 1979 and 1980: same man, different function each time. Ronald Reagan had been to Fondis County and campaigned a total of six times before his first win for the Presidency! Remarkable, Ulises realized. Fondis County was not terribly accessible to a busy candidate, and he knew that although the County Party could donate generously to a candidate, that the donations were not that large. No wonder people like Lawrence were disgusted with the current state of the Party. They'd truly believed.

Lawrence and Ronnie watched a couple of crime dramas and the evening news on television, paying close attention to the weather. "Hey—tomorrow you don't need to wear the sweater!" Lawrence announced. "At least in the afternoon. What do you think of that?"

Ronnie just smiled.

"It's gonna' be a big day tomorrow," Lawrence mused. "Gotta' be up before five to check the momma cows. I'd better lay another sweater by for you." He chose one with yellow stripes and put it next to Ronnie. "Good night, Ronnie," he whispered affectionately before turning out the light.

"It's not just spring," Diana said over their first cup of coffee that Sunday morning. "I know something's bugging you. What is it, Ul?"

"It's—something I found in a scrapbook at Headquarters. Did you know Ronald Reagan visited here six times before he became President? If that happened now, I'd be flabbergasted."

"When?"

"Nineteen Seventy six, Seventy seven, Seventy eight, Seventy nine, and Eighty—while I was still at the Agricultural College getting my Master's."

"I was here," she said slowly, "and I don't remember it. I'd probably remember something like that."

"But there was a picture of your dad with him in Seventy-seven! You sure?"

"I'd know, wouldn't I?"

That was the reason Ulises was hammering on the door to Lawrence's house that Sunday morning after church. Besides wanting this true believer back in the Party fold, Ulises had to figure out how to entice the current Republican candidate to come to the County.

He tried the door: it opened soundlessly.

With a feeling of mounting dread, he checked the ground floor. Nothing. He took the stairs, two at a time, and opened the doors at the top. Nothing. Nothing. The third door yielded to reveal a large figure standing above a body in bed.

"Hey!" Ulises yelled, running in and tackling the figure with all his might. They both hit the wall hard and Ulises saw stars. The figure he'd tackled, in a large red wool sweater, made no move. It just grinned. Ulises, shaking his head to clear it, realized that he'd tackled and probably irreparably crumpled a lifesize cardboard cutout of Ronald Reagan, fortieth President of the United States, who his wife affectionately called "Ronnie."

Summer

LESSONS IN CRYSTAL GAZING

Epona Maris

"See the images in the crystal," she says
As I shift the Smoky Quartz about,
Searching for angles that show patterns.
"I see stone," I say.
Her answer is: "Look deeper."

I have no patience for crystal gazing,
So she sets me to unraveling the twisted knots
Of the yarn she spins
And lets fall carelessly across the floor.
"Look again, look deeper."
I see reflected light, no revelations.

I remember walking as a child, along a dirt road at night,
With the sense of someone behind me.
I turned to see the grass in the barrow ditch shivering,
Spirit moving across the face of the leafy water.
I heard bells in the distance, voices in the wind.
I wrote poetry that flowed and my soul shook
As I walked the narrow road between joy and sorrow.

Now, grown up, others rely upon me,
The steady force in shifting times.
I have no time, no time to write poetry,
No time to listen to the wind.
Time to get tired but no time to rest,
No time to feel beyond my frustration.
I hear no voices in the wind,
See no spirit in the grass. No spirit.

I want to remember life beyond the material world.
I pretend the seals in the zoo are selkies,
Fields of grass are sea in a landlocked world.
I have a longing for beyond.
I feel the poetry rising in me again.

I want to learn to see auras and fairies
dancing in the garden.
I want to see visions in the crystal.
I want to hear the voices calling to me from the twilight.
I want but I don't know how to have what I want.
My thoughts turn in spirals above my heart.
"Look again, look deeper."
I am already delusional, so why can't I learn to hallucinate?
I see my eye looking at me, thinking.
I am thinking too much.

Days are filled with doing things, getting things done,
Never quite doing enough but always moving,
Until it all ends in sleep.
I wake in the night to see a hedgehog
Sitting on the bed, watching me.
I reach out a hand, it passes through him as he disappears.
"So you're not real," I tell him,
He whispers: "But I am."

I close my eyes.
I see emerald lights turning like a triskele,
I see a unicorn, faerie wings, a snake twining
through a sheaf of wheat:
A bowl of visions that hold the meaning I give to them.
"Look again, look deeper."

I want to be wiser than my fear.
I want to shine through the stone
that life has built around me,
I want to sing with the voices I hear in the distance.
I pause to breathe, feel the energy flow from my hands.
"Look again, look deeper," I hear her say with my voice.
I look again and see myself:

>   Deeper than a well of stars.

XIII.

WHO I REALLY AM

Deirdre H. Moon

It's hot and I seek out the air conditioning at the Fondis Soda Shoppe just around the corner from the bank. Lime soda with chocolate ice cream, made the old fashioned way, soothes my temperament.

"Hey, Deirdre," a voice summons. I twirl on the counter seat and nod at Sunny, a newcomer to the local womyn's group. Sunshine McCloud heard about Fondis back in New York and came out here to check it out. I like her but feel so grouchy because of the heat that I'm not sure I'll be good company.

A faerie tweaks a curl escaping my bandana. Okay. I get it.

"Join me," I call out as Sunny looks hesitant. She rewards me with an instant smile, pushes her sleek blonde hair back into a pony tail and slips a scrunchie off her wrist to secure the golden fall of hair. I wonder if it's difficult to be that beautiful all the time.

Sunny orders a diet soda and glances at me with a shrug. "I'm on a diet. I'm always on a diet. I'm trying to get an agent here in Fondis. It's harder than in New York. But the editor of the *Fondly Fondis* monthly magazine asked me to pose for the cover so maybe that will help." I nod. She lives in a world out of my ken.

"So, what do you do, Deirdre?" she asks and slips the paper cover off a red straw.

"I live in a yurt up on the bluff overlooking the Bijou. Me and my critters. Come visit sometime." I want to be hospitable. She can tell I'm hedging. Sometimes I get away with misdirection but she's honing in for real information.

"I'd love to. What kind of work do you do?" She has piercing blue eyes.

"Well, I do a number of things and it's hard to explain."

"Try me." Again that fabulous smile. Maybe I have seen her on the cover of magazines, now that I think about it.

"Okay. I hold the energy for the Western Quadrant of Protection in the Fondis Energy Circle under the guidance of the Overlighting Deva of the Universe." Usually when I tell people the truth, they laugh and we start talking about Star Trek. She doesn't laugh.

"Wow. What kind of energy?"

I level with her. "Originally, I'm from Sirius and when I meditate, and even when I don't, I'm guided by Sirian energies that alter my DNA as necessary. That way I can maintain my presence in the human form and be of service to the planet. I really love it here."

She pushes away the diet drink and signals the soda jerk. (Yes, old fashioned soda jerk. The local high school kids love getting this job.)

"Give me what she's having." She points at my frothy libation. "I knew I was supposed to come in here today, Deirdre. I get so caught up out there in the fashion world and all the phony hoopdedoo. I'm not sure what you're talking about, but I went to a palm reader in the East Village before I left New York. She told me I'd meet someone like you. Bright red hair, wild green eyes and a non-conformist. She said I was to study with you." Sunny looks earnestly at me and turns to the sip the foam off the top of her lime soda with chocolate ice cream.

I don't want any students. Drat. I suppose she went to my Aunt Red Palm who refuses to come to Colorado. Says her work is down there in the village. I always like visiting her. Now she's sending me her people. It's probably part of my assignment. I'll have to talk to She Who Knows All and the Lady of the Lake, two other women who hold energy on the Fondis Wheel.

"Join me for Solstice," I say, keeping my doubts to myself. The light of day and night can balance and so can I. Really.

XIV.

FAIR: HONEST; DECENT.

Roger Rural

Fair: *(n) 1. An improvised activity involving County Commissioners, dust, a queen, dust, lots of animals and volunteers, and dust; 2. The best choice, no matter how hard; 3. What a little girl looks like under a bonnet; 4. When your four year-old screams: "That's not Fair!" in January, you can reply: "No; it isn't until early August."*

You can tell which animals at the Fair haven't been worked with merely by watching them in the show ring. If the 4-H owner hasn't worked with her goat, heifer, sheep, or pig, the spectators know it almost immediately, as does the judge, in ring center, because the animal's skittish. It will respond to the prod or the leash; but cautiously, because it does not trust its owner. The animal will perform, but almost resentfully; doing what it is expected to do, but no more. That's because the owner hasn't really taken the time to really understand the animal: its quirks and its gifts.

After having worked with goats for a number of years, I already know, in general, what all are capable of; and, in general, what their limitations are.

Characteristically, for instance, I expect that they'll come to me when I've got a bucket of grain for them, but they will back away if I approach them with a leash or a rope. Individually, I know some of them love to be scratched behind their ears, and one of them loves to listen to my rendition of hit songs from 1928, like "Button Up Your Overcoat," and "Sweet Sue; Just You." Because I understand their likes and dislikes and have taken time to appreciate them, they "perform" for me by making my job around here easier. How easy? I know what they'll put up with.

A lot of employees are that way: they want to be appreciated by their bosses for their talents and abilities; otherwise, they won't perform to the best expectation. A good boss needs to know which employees are willing to work for a little encouragement and which ones will perform without much encouragement; what concerns they have, and what they can perform.

It took close to forever to get our big goat to accept harness for the goat cart I'd ordered especially for him. The goat kept backing up until I started scratching his ear and singing: "How would you like to swing on a star?/ Carry moonbeams home in a jar?" Probably the shock of a Bing Crosby song coupled with traditional labor shocked the goat out of his stubbornness.

Maybe it was the scratch behind the ear I gave him before each of his tasks: Whatever it was, he performed beautifully when we offered rides for four year-olds around the firehouse throughout the course of a spring Sunday afternoon. I knew he loved the singing and I knew he loved the grain I gave him after each turn. He worked for me because he understood that I wanted him to and would serve him with a reward.

Employees aren't much different, really. They want the same feeling of reward and they want to know what they can do to be appreciated. A good animal owner works with the animals; a good boss works with the employees. A mutual interest in doing a good job is shared by owner and animal; between employer and employee. They have a loyalty to one another as a consequence. If the boss decides not to let the employee share in doing the good job or considers the employee irrelevant to what he is trying to do, however, the employee resents it, and rightly so.

If I expected my large goat to perform, then did not feed him, he'd probably not perform a second time. If a boss expects my time, my work, and my devotion, then does not reward me with appreciation or cash for a job well done, I'm not interested in doing the job a second time.

Most 4-H contestants understand this basic principle. Funny that a lot of other people, when dealing with each other, in marriage, parenthood, county government, or jobs, don't.

XV.

FONDIS ETIQUETTE

Epona Maris

I used to wonder why bartenders stand behind bars. It seemed like it must be for punishment or protection, but observation has taught me that it has more to do with the maintenance of ritual boundaries.

Another geometric phenomenon that has fascinated me is the marking of new tire ruts after it rains on our dirt roads. Shortly after the next rainstorm you can count for yourself. Even though the average car has tires on two sides, and most roads allow traffic in two directions, the number of tracks drawn into the mud will be three. Of course, roads nearer to the city might not conform to this pattern. I spend far too much time contemplating such things.

The Fondis Bar has always been known as just the Fondis Bar, despite frequent change of ownership. Each owner seems to feel the need to stamp his or her imprint on the bar by changing the official name, but, since ownership changes hands more often than trees change leaves, the locals stick to the basics to avoid confusion.

Most owners seem to think they have some control of the place, but in reality they're down the line from the bartender, the driver of the delivery truck, and Johnny B. Goode, the rattlesnake that has lived beneath the front steps for more years than I can remember. Why a bar should have steps outside the door is another thing that puzzles me, given the athletic ability of its usual patrons.

On the night I had the most reason to question the existence of steps at the bar door, I had wandered in looking for conversation. Phillip was tending bar, so I asked for a mixed drink just so I could watch his graceful hands create it. He is a pleasant conversationalist, due in part to his beautiful baritone voice. He had been a professional opera singer out east before coming home to Fondis to help his mother through breast cancer.

Dan was one of the few people sharing the bar, since it was early on a long summer evening. Dan is tall and burly, usually dressed in biker leathers with his hair tied in a graying braid under his cap. He has a striking tattoo of an eagle tearing apart an anatomically correct human heart on his right shoulder and another of the horned moon of the Goddess on his left. He was sipping Fondis Memories, a local microbrew, while talking with Roger Rural and a young man I didn't recognize.

They were arguing, rather, so I stepped closer to hear it. A good argument in a bar is a wonderful spectator sport. They were arguing about politics, however, a difficult topic to argue with style. Dan turned to me to get my opinion on the value of individual participation in the political process. It seemed that the stranger was disparaging it.

"I think it's of the utmost importance for individuals to actively participate in politics," I said. "Otherwise we would leave the poor souls we elect to the mercy of the political virus." The stranger looked perplexed, or that might have been the effects of the standard American pee-beer he was drinking. Roger was drinking oatmeal stout.

"There is a virus," I explained, "that was first identified in Washington, D.C. but has since been found spreading throughout the country. It generally only infects holders of political office, but can be contagious to people who seek office, as well." I was performing my best professorial act by that point, and the stranger looked even more perplexed. Dan just belched.

"It hides in the brain and eats at the neurons. After a few years in office even smart people with good common sense start acting like fools. If we aren't careful, the damage can be permanent. That usually occurs by the end of a second term in office."

The stranger looked skeptical. "So what do you do to prevent that?" he asked.

"Why, vote them out, of course. Or pass term limitation laws, but that can give us the false sense that we no longer have to worry about this problem."

Roger nodded his head in agreement, "Here in Fondis," he added sagely, "we are very conscious of the dangers of the political virus and remain vigilant. We take good care of those who sacrifice themselves for local political office and make sure that none ever serves a second term. In fact, there are groups of dedicated citizens that are ready to start recall petitions the day after elections, no matter which candidate wins."

For some reason the stranger chose to turn back to Dan to continue the argument, but the topic soon shifted to the importance of supporting our troops in Iraq. Dan was doing a fine job of arguing the point that supporting the troops and supporting the war could reasonably be considered two separate concepts. The stranger was not holding up his end of the argument well: he just kept restating his belief that it was "un-American" to voice opinions against the war because that could harm troop morale.

I have always enjoyed a well-reasoned argument, but have a reason for disliking a poorly presented one. Years ago, while walking meditatively in the woods near midnight I stumbled across the faerie mound west of town, disrupting the fair folk's dancing. I have since made up with them and am welcome to drop by at almost any time, but, since I had completely destroyed a particularly beautiful dance pattern, they were mad enough to seek retribution.

Dancing is more important to fey folk than football or baseball is to a sports fan. The fey choreographer whipped me three times with her rowan wand, leaving interesting scars on my shins, but that wasn't enough to cool her blood. Since I was loudly defending my innocence in the matter, she determined that my penalty, or *geas*, for my boorish clumsiness was that I can never pass by an unequal argument. No matter my own opinion on the topic, I am compelled to argue for the side that is least well defended. I must say that I have developed a skill for it, over the years.

I therefore proceeded to argue the stranger's point that public criticism of the war amounts to a dangerous lack of support for our troops. I waxed eloquent about the psychological state of our country and the consequences of losing resolve in midcourse of a war. Dan knows me well, so he just drank his beer as he prepared a counter-offensive. Roger added a couple of fine points to round out my thesis, but generally stuck to his stout, waiting to judge the full effect. The stranger, however, was not used to the intricacies of Fondis debate. That must be why he shoved me back on my stool and commenced to insult Dan about his lack of manly military ideals.

Dan interpreted this as an attack on his experience as a platoon leader in Viet Nam and demonstrated his feelings about it by towering above the stranger. An image of dirt roads after a rainstorm came to my mind: I could tell that they were on track for a head-on collision and neither would be courteous enough to drift to the side of the road so the other could pass.

That was the point that Phillip, as a skilled bartender, chose to intervene. He placed his hands firmly on the bar and breathed deeply. The voice that emerged from his diaphragm would have pleased Pavarotti. "If you can't conduct a civilized argument, then get the hell out of my bar," he intoned. The echoes danced among the cavernous rafters.

I was startled at first, but determined that, since I was capable of civilized argumentation, I had no need to leave. Roger was in no danger, of course, and Dan must have reached a similar conclusion, since he sat back down on his stool. The stranger, however, must have realized his insufficiencies, or perhaps he was overwhelmed by the resonance of Phillip's voice. Either way, he chose to stalk dramatically to the door.

"You're all a bunch of communist queers," he declaimed, then turned to make a dramatic exit. Unfortunately for him, Johnny B. Goode had crawled out from under the steps to see what the fuss was all about. He graciously warned the stranger of his presence on the step by rattling his tail. Leaving the scene, the stranger made a leap that would have impressed the faeries.

"I guess he doesn't understand Fondis etiquette," Roger said. Phillip just shrugged gracefully and poured him another stout. We settled in for a pleasant evening chat.

XVI.

AN ART BOOK, 4-H, AND THE USES OF MEMORY

Roger Rural

"Depending on whose memory you may employ,
He was a greater man who came of a great boy."
(attr. To the poet, T. Chumondley Frink, from Babbitt, *by Sinclair Lewis)*

G. Sibley Haycock's 4-volume Desk Composition Series, published in 1904, not only gives rules for capitalization, spelling, and punctuation: it also includes rules for writing well, most of which boil down to "imitate the masters."

In volume IV of this set, measuring five inches high, three inches across and three inches deep, designed to sit inconspicuously on a typist's small desk or unobtrusively on a railway clerk's shelf, is a series of prose examples, ranging from The Sermon on the Mount to Robert Louis Stevenson's "The King of the Golden River." Knowing that his 1904 audience would be chiefly male, Haycock took great pains to include "the finest example of direct prose available," then quotes Hamlet's soliloquy on death. One wonders if an aspiring certified public accountant, taking Haycock to heart, would devise a letter to a coal dealer:

"Dear Sir:
To sleep, to dream—aye! There's the rub! Four more tons of coal is required so Not be poor in spirit, I, and so—end it all.
                To make of so long a life,
                Signature."

Mr. Stritch, the Math teacher, striving for an elegance not found in everyday life, takes the equation for triangles, A squared, plus B squared equals C squared, and makes it almost holy: like communion for the first time after a long catechism. This truth, which Pythagoras and Euclid were convinced was delivered from heaven, truly could solve the problems of the universe. It is an attitude that has been mocked by our European cousins, world-weary and ironic; too full of high purpose and therefore, vague.

In horsemanship competition contestants not only need to know how to ride well and in certain patterns: they must also know such arcana as to what size shoe the horse wears, what is considered proper grooming, and what importance a certain mixture of grains has on the horse's diet. It's a wonderful, sensible, "can-do" format, that, once learned, can be applied to any other area, the same way knowledge of triangles can; the same way G. Sibley Haycock's work can.

It's the same way with Goats. "Why do I need to know all this stuff?" Raul complained to me the other day. At age thirteen, he's heavily into teenage sports, some of which include stubbornness and whining. "I'm never going to raise goats or have anything to do with them in my future!"

"You know this stuff so you won't be embarrassed when the judge asks you a question," I explained quietly, "in the same way that you know you have to look pleasant and confident in the ring even when you don't feel like it. The acquisition of the knowledge is what's valuable, Raul."

Rachel, who has just completed Kindergarten, was given a blank cardboard-sided Composition Book on her first day of school. Then she was instructed to choose a laminated card from a pile, all bearing photos of animals, on the teacher's desk, copy it onto a page assiduously, taking care to copy the text below the picture, then turn the page, find another card, and continue the process.

"Koala bears are small marsupials that live in Australia, chiefly in Eucalyptus trees. They measure two to three feet long, have sharp claws, and are tailless. They look like small, grey bears."

The first exercise took her the greater part of a week, one hour each day, laboriously copying. Then she was urged to copy another card into her Composition Book. By year's end, "Daddy, I got every animal in my Book except the elephant and the killer whale."

She also can recognize words like "marsupial," "eucalyptus," "Australia," and dozens of others. She will be writing sentences, soon; maybe about such things, maybe not.

When my son recognizes that the arcane knowledge he has picked up while learning about goats, his appearance with goats, and his ability to control goats transfers to whatever skills he employs without goats, he'll recognize what G. Sibley Haycock, Euclid, Mr. Stritch, and those who founded 4-H understood: Success is the acquisition and the employment of the knowledge; not the knowledge itself.

XVII.

ASTROLOGICAL MUMBO JUMBO

Deirdre H. Moon

Weirdful, that's what I am.

Closely related to wonderful and weird but a superb synergy that draws up the vision on a full moon night. It also hums along on the long rays of Lugh claiming the noonday skies as we hone in on Summer Solstice.

Weirdful might just leap out of your heart and make you want to dance and sing if you're wandering in Fondis during the Mother Cross sky transit on June 8.

I was dancing and singing without any explanation at all when I happened on Cassandra the astrologer at the used bookstore just off the main drag.

Now you don't get a chance at all to talk or ask a question when that willowy sky woman with violet eyes starts talking. Conjunct this and retrograde that. I can't keep up so I can't quote her but it goes something like this.

Sun, Venus and Mercury are in Gemini and the Moon and Uranus in Pisces with Jupiter in Virgo and Pluto in Sag equals the Mother Cross. Got it? Plus Venus eclipses the sun so your heart may just be opening at this very moment.

Well, if you're not into astrological mumbo jumbo, don't worry. You don't have to understand it, or quote it or believe in it. It just happens anyway. Whether you're cruising Fondis or not.

"But Cassandra, it all sounds so complicated. What does it mean for me?" Of course, it's all about me.

"Worry not, Deirdre, my little Aquarian chickadee, you get it when you don't get it." She turned, paid cash for a stack of books. Layers of gauzy skirts shimmered as she opened the door. Pausing, she turned back and smiled, one of those all time smiles that let's you know she's something special, you're something special. "And don't forget to wear a weirdful costume for the Solstice parade. But you always do." And she drifted into the late afternoon sunlight.

I glanced down at the T-shirt knotted at my waist, the slogan reads "Question Authority". My tie-dye skirt falls just above tattoos on my ankles. Toe rings balance my masculine and feminine nature. I catch my image in the glass of the side window, see the dangle of my earrings, the sparkle of my nose ring, the wildness of my hair.

Weirdful I am and more so as the planets shift and I consider a costume for the Solstice parade. I'll hike up to the ridge in search of the unicorn and see if he'd like to prance down the parade route with me on his back. His golden horn will glisten in the long rays of sunshine. Maybe I'll wear that hand-woven burnoose and harem pants with my purple pointy-toed shoes.

If you're walking in Fondis and miss any of these fabulous places it may simply be the blanket of miller moths that obscures your vision.

XVIII.

THE LESSON OF GEESE

Epona Maris

I have a fondness for geese that I find hard to explain. Not just the part about the hissing, honking, biting and wing-battering, but the connection to Faerie they have for me. Not to mention it was a pair of geese that turned my life around. Life in Fondis tends to happen that way.

I was in 4H the majority of my youth, and it tended to be a humbling experience. The judges never seemed interested in the areas where I had some small talent. There was no class for fermenting beverages, a pride of mine. And at the horse show there was no class for bareback, barefoot and halter. I love goats, but could never bring myself to trim their tails to the skin except for a bush at the tip. A goat is not a poodle. Even when I tried to conform I failed: everybody and her brother seemed to bring a market turkey to show and mine never placed higher than fifth. But it was in the poultry barn during my penultimate 4H year that I had my epiphany.

Amy Johnson brought a goose that year. Amy was a prissy snob whose parents bought her whatever she wanted. Even though she had won Grand Champion for her Rhode Island Red hen, and Reserve Champion for her lamb, not to mention her Grand Champion dress that she later wore to prom just before marrying her high school sweetheart, that wasn't enough for her. She brought a Toulouse gander, a fine looking fellow with an evil temper. Since it was the only goose, it obviously won first place. I had never even won a second place ribbon in all my years of trying. Suddenly it all came together for me: lack of competition leads to winning. Amy was a senior that year and wouldn't be back. No one else seemed impressed by the noisy, foul-mouthed bird, so the field would be mine, next year, given a bit of planning.

The two fuzzy goslings arrived the next spring and spent their first weeks in a box by the woodstove. My parents were tolerant, if not very attentive. Eventually the gangly teenaged goose and gander made their way out to a pen in the backyard. Each morning I would open the pen gate to let them forage in the yard. At first they came tumbling out, tripping over their oversize feet, but, as their wing feathers grew, they learned grace. Since they were Pilgrim geese, the gander was pure white while the goose was a soft gray. Each morning as I let them out, they would run with their wings spread into the rising sun, glowing like pearls. At night I would herd them back into their pen to keep them safe from coyotes, neighborhood dogs, and foxes. Given the gander's instinctive response to everything remotely new, Hissy was a natural name. But even at seventeen I was able to resist the yin/yang balance of naming the goose Missy. Her name was Esmeralda.

I have always been absent-minded: my brain is often somewhere other than the practical realms of thought. This happens most often at twilight, as the boundaries between day and night fade and all things become one. In the summertime I have always loved to walk through the hills above Fondis at sunset, watching as the trees pattern the light into characters that I can almost read. I am still trying to learn that language.

One evening shortly before fair time that summer, instead of feeding the geese I found myself wandering among the trees, pondering such teenage mysteries as the nature of infinity and why all the popular kids hated me. Twilight is when the walls between worlds become thin and one can sometimes catch glimpses beyond our reality. I was paying little attention to reality at that time, of course, so I had no idea where I was when the flickering lights started to swirl around me. Mesmerized by them, I didn't see the dancers until I tripped over them.

I rolled over, rubbing my elbow, to see my gesture mirrored by a black-haired, emerald-eyed beauty on the ground beside me. I noticed that she was only wearing a feather skirt and a few flowers before I noticed the gauzy wings. It was a minute or two later before I realized that she was a good bit shorter than I was. Granted, most people are, but usually not by four feet or so.

"What?" I managed to say. She grinned at me.

"If you can't learn to keep your head in one world or another, you had better learn to expect surprises, "she said. Her voice was beautiful, too.

"My mother said something like that when I tripped over the pig I was feeding," I answered. She laughed, rose gracefully to her feet and held out her hand.

"You'd best get up before Mistress Grisena catches you here. This is her moondance you just interrupted," my companion said. I didn't expect her to be able to help me up, but I quickly found myself on my feet. A good thing it was, too, since I was now confronted by someone just as short but armed with a wicked stick. My shins are still marked by it.

"Five centuries of perfection ruined by one clumsy human," Mistress Grisena shrieked. Even as I backed up, I was impressed by her operatic skills.

I tried apologizing, explained that I meant no harm, that I was only meditating as I walked and had no idea that I was interrupting an event of such importance, but she cut me short with another switch. That touched right to my deep-down sense of justice. This was a free country and I had just as much right to trespass on someone else's private property as they did. I told her as much, with all the eloquence I could quickly dredge up.

"Enough!" she commanded. "You like to argue, do you?" I thought of denying it, but felt it was self evident. "Well then," she said with a satisfied tone that sent goose bumps up my arms, "argue you shall, henceforth at each opportunity you are given. But never the easy path: you must choose the side least well defended. And you may never decline the challenge. So shall it be."

With that benediction, she pointed her wand at me and something inside of me changed. Or, perhaps, didn't change, but surfaced. Despite the complications, it has not been the worst curse I have been given.

At the time, however, I was more interested in getting out of reach of her wand, so I accepted with relief when the faerie I had stumbled over offered to show me the way home. "Better than letting Mistress Grisena notice the condition of my skirt," she said as she rose into the air. Its feathers were a bit ragged where I had stepped on them. I had to jog to keep up with her flitting among the trees, but managed to apologize as I more properly made her acquaintance. "My name is Epona Maris," I said, sticking out my hand. "Sorry about the feathers." She laughed as she swept my hand with her wings.

"Horse of the Sea, you are, or at least your feet move like a horse at sea!" She paused and dipped lightly in the air. "My name is Showelreth Foxfire," she said. "You can call on me and perhaps I will answer."

We were at the forest edge near my home. I could see the predawn mist shiver as a breeze tickled it over the grass. I turned back to thank her, but saw only the brush of a fox's tail as it disappeared between the trees. Thinking of foxes made me remember my geese and the fact that I had not returned them to their pen before my absent-minded walk last evening. I ran to the backyard and called to them.

At first there was no answer, but then I heard a faint honking from under the house deck. I reached under it and felt feathers. Esmeralda was unhurt but she tucked her head into my armpit as I held her close. "Where is Hissy?" I asked her, but she didn't answer. There were drops of blood on the ground and white feathers scattered about.

I sat holding Esmeralda and mentally kicking myself as the sun rose. My shoulder hurt from falling, my shins were starting to crust with drying blood and my muscles were tight with cold, but my heart hurt worse. At that moment, Hissy and Esmeralda meant far more than a ribbon at fair. I rested my cheek on her soft gray feathers and stared into the glowing sun until it fractured through my tears.

The sun rays moved suddenly and grew shining wings that flapped in the mist, accompanied by the sound of escaping steam. Hissy walked up to Esmeralda and me, head lowered and neck shaking. He was muddy and missing feathers, but still very much alive. Tangled in what was left of his wing feathers was a leather cord with red-gold fox hairs tied to it. I put the cord around my neck and gave thanks to my faerie friend as I thought of her dancing in a lovely skirt of white goose feathers.

The 4H judge frowned at Hissy's missing feathers, but grudgingly awarded me a blue ribbon at fair. That evening, as the moon rose, I tied the ribbon on a branch at the edge of the forest. By morning it was gone.

XIX.

ON THE PRIMORDIAL SEA FLOOR

Roger Rural

PRIMORDIAL: *(adj)* 1. *Pertaining to the time when your father was young;* 2. *Describing a particularly Neanderthal sort of fellow one meets in Single's Bars;* 3. *"Primeordeal," in a Texas Steak House, usually means eating as much prime rib as one can hold.*

There's an archaeology to our Fondis back yard and sometimes, paleontology. Children insure the former; dogs, the latter; and when one digs a hole, both come into play.

About five hundred million years ago, when my backyard was under water, the only thing that the elements seemed to leave was a lot of fine sand, which remained long after the ice caps formed at the poles and the inland sea receded.

We have 27 broiler chicks, 10 Bantam chicks, 10 laying chicks, and 6 turkey poults: all about five weeks old, now living in the basement. The heater is cranked to ninety degrees Fahrenheit and the shoplights we employ for closer heat and an illusion of the sun are on 18 hours a day in the cages.

It's the greatest number we've ever raised at one time. That's why I'm digging holes in the primordial seabed: to plant posts for fences and gates.

"Can't mix chickens until they're old," is a Country saying pertaining to social norming among children, but it's especially true of most fowl. When we move the laying chickens out to the large chicken yard, we draw a strong gate behind them and plug any holes above or below because it's the natural tendency of roosters to dominate a flock, and new arrivals are considered a threat.

A few years ago, in my naivete, I mixed some young chickens and roosters with the more mature flock and found their bodies, pecked to death, in the corner of the coop, the next day.

Rachel, after strenuous labor with shovel and hand at the hole I'd assigned her, held up a flat bone, about four inches in length and an inch high. "Was this a prehistoric fish, daddy?" she asked in her six year-old quaver.

"No. I think it was a pot roast from last year. Cattle. Beef."

"And this?" She held up a metal sugar bowl; the mud clinging to it.

"Sugarbowl, Rachel. A legacy of the children who played here before."

"Where are they now?"

"Probably all grown up," I remarked. "I suppose, enrolled in college. If a little girl of six lived here when we moved in, fourteen years ago, she'd be twenty by now."

"But what about the other children?"

"Don't know. They had ten month-old twins when they moved out. Those boys would be about fifteen, now."

Fifteen from six is a lifetime when viewed from the narrow end of the telescope, and it gave Rachel pause. "So everybody grows up?" she asked.

"Yes; everybody does. Even your father."

The new turkeys will occupy a small yard we've just built. The broiler chickens will live their temporary lives of six months in the old Greenhouse. The new laying chickens will live behind the stout gate. Everything will follow its natural, anthropological, paleontological course: on the sands of the primordial sea.

XX.

FOURTH OF JULY

Deirdre H. Moon

Everyone's eyes followed the parade except mine. I was people watching. Fourth of Julys melt into themselves, year after year, parade after parade, endless memories of sky vision fireworks merging.

I rode my mountain bike down the rough trails of the Bijou to attend the festivities that morning, first stopping off to see Cerridwen. She wasn't in the barn milking goats so I climbed the stile and walked between pines as morning shadows lapped the path. I was dazed with the ephemeral mists of dawn magic. I found Cerridwen at the Medicine Wheel.

Bringing my attention back as the holiday revelers hooted, I sighed at the contrast. My eyes roved the crowd absently and stopped abruptly as they rested on the tall stranger across the street. Piercing blue eyes below heavy brows, both shadowed by the rim of his hat. Even a day old growth of beard did not diminish the strong line of his jaw.

Over the cacophony of the parade I heard the whir of a hummingbird above my head. I smiled hearing Cerridwen's voice remind me that that the tiny bird was the symbol for the nectar of life.

The princess of Fondis rode by, resplendent on her sleek palomino, her pale yellow satin skirts spread over the horse's rump. I looked at the crowd across the street, searching for the blue eyed man but he was gone. Just another stranger in the crowd.

"Deirdre." A deep voice spoke at my shoulder. I turned and looked into probing blue eyes. How'd he get through the crowd and across the street? I followed him down the alley between the hotel and the malt shop, away from the din of the celebration.

"How do you know me?" I'm usually suspect of men wearing ironed jeans but was willing to overlook that bias for the fit of them.

"I read your writing. Someone forwards it to me in cyberspace." I grinned at the compliment.

"What's your name?"

"Finn." It sounded familiar.

"Where are you from?" He had a slight brogue.

"Orcas Island for the moment. And I have to leave now." He reached into a shirt pocket and handed me an iridescent scalloped sea shell. "Come see me," he said.

I studied the shell and frowned. When I looked up, he was gone.

Wandering back to the parade, I was just in time to catch the mayor's shining black carriage, pulled by two equally shiny black percherons, come to a halt. The mayor stood and motioned for silence. Someone handed him a Fosters and he raised it high as the crowd cheered. Glugging down half of it, he shouted "Vote for me in the primary next month." The carriage lurched forward and he sat abruptly. Mrs. Mayor dabbed a white hankie to his chin.

Fourth of July isn't just about independence. It's also about inter-dependence. I thought of my old crone friend Cerridwen, of the hummingbird and the princess and the new blue eyed friend and the sea shell in my palm. I'd look at a map to find that island in search of his blue eyes.

XXI.

THE LANGUAGE OF ANIMALS

Epona Maris

Most of us have wondered about what animals are saying to each other as they go about their busy days. Since most of our days seem even busier than theirs, we rarely pursue that thought. Practicing the art of deep listening can bring interesting rewards for those who take the time.

I have always been fascinated by the language of Crows. At first, I puzzled over what they were saying to each other in their sonorous voices, but I learned the clue to translate crow talk when I realized that they are Buddhists. Crows love to draw attention to the moment: "Be Here Now, Here, Now" they caw to each other from the treetops. Then they practice their walking meditations as they carefully attend to the roadside suffering of the world.

Sparrows and Finches, on the other hand, live for gossip. "Did you see? Did you see? Did you see?" one will twitter to a neighbor as they flit from branch to branch. Sometimes the whole bush will twitter with silliness. In their own way, they also live for the moment.

Hawks keep a careful watch on the past, however. "Freeeeee" they call, "stay free," as they remind us of what could happen if we lose vigilance. Hawks keep careful tally of the injustices of the past; they are as detail oriented as accountants. Eagles, on the other hand, are big-picture thinkers, gliding high over the past, present and future without much care as to which is which.

A Meadowlark will waver between asserting his territory and boasting of its benefits. "This spot is mine, mine," they sing, ending with a trill of "and a beautiful spot it is!" Warblers just give themselves over to hedonism: "It's a glorious, wonderful, beautiful day, it is, yes it is!"

Domestic fowl are expressive sorts, from the "Here, here, here," checking in of Turkeys as they scavenge the yard, to the "look what I did!" pride of Chickens laying eggs. Geese are the experts at expression of outraged sensibilities as they comment on any lesser animal's barnyard faux pas: "What was that?" they honk in their loudest, deepest voice, "you did what?"

Dogs, like most mammals, are quite capable of a wide variety of vocal expressions, not to mention their versatile body language, yet when they get irritated they are as inexpressive as the rest of us.

I often listen through my open window, late into the summer nights, as they patrol their perimeters and report to each other their findings. "What, what, what?" they bark to each other as the Coyotes on the hilltops fall over themselves with giggles: "You fools, you fools," the Coyotes laugh, until boredom overtakes them and they melt into the stillness of the night.

XXII.

FASHION AND THE PIGYARD

Roger Rural

Fashion: *(n)* 1. What is trendy; 2. Something guys over age 40 ignore; 3. Not to be confused with fascism, though the two are sometimes similar.

    COLLEAGUES! The memorandum read in larger and more intrusive type than that accorded a search warrant, THE SUMMER READERS' GROUP IS STARTING MAY FIRST THIS YEAR AND WE WANT YOUR INPUT!
    PLEASE LIST YOUR FAVORITE BOOK, SUBMIT IT, AND WE WILL CONTACT YOU! WE LOVE NEW MEMBERS!
    So I listed my favorite book, submitted it, and waited. That was two years ago. Save for a few wayward looks and some giggles, I have not been contacted for membership, discussion of my favorite book, or reasons why it is my favorite book. That's because the book's not fashionable.
    "I want to completely pull out this fence," I told my eleven year-old son, "and replace it with something more permanent and lasting, which means we need to dig the ground for wooden posts approximately three feet apart. It will make a better pigyard."
    My son leaned on his shovel and shook his head. "Really?" he asked.
    The duplex where my friend Annette lived, on Detroit Street, in Denver, had a shared front porch and two doors. Annette and her mother lived on the north side; her grandmother lived on the south side. When one entered Annette's side, one was immediately confronted by a large round coffee table, behind which sat an enormous Chesterfield sofa: one of those six foot high leather jobbers that measured a good eight feet in length and three in width: perfectly suitable for a downtown men's club of high ceilings and cigar smoke and pool tables, but not customary in a room that measured ten by ten.
    Seated crosslegged in its middle was Annette, who said, in a solemn voice, "Climb aboard. We're about to go to Mozambique; then on to Madagascar." That morning, we piloted the Mediterranean, sped across the North Atlantic, went through the Straits of Gibraltar, and ventured near

Tierra Del Fuego. "I've read National Geographic," she confided, "and I know all about these places. In Tierra Del Fuego, they don't wear shirts." I nodded. I was all of nine years old. Around us was the world; not a small black and white TV set crammed amidst a few volumes and dozens of issues of magazines: Family Circle, Reader's Digest, National Geographic *among them, bunched against the far wall. Behind us was the coast of Sierra Leone, or the shores of Ithaca; not a poky little hallway leading to a bathroom and two bedrooms. Space was Annette's to command, and she did so masterfully. I was all of four feet tall; I suppose she was, too; but the Chesterfield sofa felt like a luxury ocean liner.*

I'd gotten it into my head that the pigs needed more space, even though six at a time had been raised in the same pigyard, year after year, and seemed to have little trouble with the 18 x 20 feet of space they had on the lee side of the barn, sheltering in their secondhand pig house, drinking water from a used trough and eating from a feeder made out of plastic barrel halves. Everything I'd read pointed to making more space for them.

"They'll be disease-free!" the advertisement proclaimed, "and fat and healthy if you give them more beautiful space!" The ad had suggested wooden fence; a painted and more snug pig house; a much better drainage system.

"Daddy," Raul asked, "have your pigs ever had any diseases?"

"None that I can recall," I answered, enthusiastically digging at the bottom of the fence.

"And you've been raising pigs for eight years, right?"

I nodded. Almost by accident, I acquired a couple of yearling pigs and decided to fatten them up in a corner of the barnyard that only saw sun in the morning. I fed them cracked corn and goat milk and plenty of fresh water all through the summer and part of the fall. In November, I took them to the butcher, a veteran of almost forty years in processing meats of all kinds. He was amazed. "You have a gift," he told me. "Never have I seen such good organic pork!"

Annette's mother fed us lunch in due course. We'd just steamed up the Hudson and docked in Manhattan. We had toasted tomato sandwiches with lots of mayonnaise at a spare enamel table on mismatched plastic plates that we carried to the sink when done.

"You don't have much here," I observed, looking at the shelves lining the kitchen, empty, save a couple of cans of corn and green beans.

"But we don't need much; Annette and I," Annette's mother interjected. "Why have more than you need? It is unnecessary!" She imperiously waved her hand. "Why have things that cannot be used?"

"So you want to turn this pig yard into Disneyland?" Raul asked me with all the sarcasm he could muster.

"Not Disneyland," I replied patiently. "I just want a space for the pigs to be healthy and well before I take them to slaughter."

"No offense, but what if it works already?" he asked.

I looked at the tired old pigyard: the used pig house; the feeder and trough. The ground was certainly well-trampled, but snow and rain had rid it of disease.

When I returned home from Annette's, I asked my mother if I could go back.

"We'll see," she answered. She was sitting on our gold and white upholstered couch, seeming miles from where I sat in our cold living room in a chair of the same heavy upholstery.

"Did you have a nice time?" she asked, her voice seeming to boom against our white textured walls, gold carpet, painted woodwork, and the wall of book bindings that provided the only color variance in the room.

"In the afternoon, while Mrs. Hill took a nap, we played in Annette's room," I reported, "and we had to get on the bed to close the door!"

"Really?" she asked, looking at her fingernails.

"And we put together puzzles all afternoon. In the morning, we played on the couch."

"Really?"

"And we had tomato sandwiches for lunch."

"Really?"

Annette told me the following Monday, "My mother says I can't play with you anymore because your mother says I'm too poor."

"Why change something that works?" Raul asked me.

Indeed. I sent him inside to find some ice cream while I shoveled the dirt I'd unearthed. Why mess with success? I was only trying to be fashionable.

64

I hope Annette is a Geography teacher or a world traveler. I do not know. She was one of those terribly bright children who appear in elementary school one year and are gone the next.

"Daddy, the pigs are going to be all right, aren't they?" Raul asked.

"Yeah," I told him heavily. "You were right; they don't need Disneyland to thrive."

"We don't need all that," Annette's mother had said, going against the fashion of many Americans, who show off plenty by having more things than they know what to do with because it's "fashionable."

There's a certain irony here: I'd told the Summer Readers' Group that my favorite book was Raising the Homestead Hog, *by Jerome D. Belanger.*

XXIII.

PIERCED

Deirdre H. Moon

"Oh, no," my friend squeals, tents her hands over her mouth in horror as she stares at me.

Oh, yes.

"I can't believe you did it." She covers her eyes, shivers.

Believe it.

"You really pierced your nose."

Yup. It all had to do with the Moon and black history. Plus I'd checked it out with my local psychic, tossed the Celtic Wisdom sticks and shuffled a couple of tarot decks. The time was right.

I mean any ol' time farmer knows you castrate and all those other blood things in the dark of the moon. So, I figure if you pierce, it better be the dark of the moon. It was.

Now, about black history. Remember Angela Davis? Black activist in the sixties? She was the first person I ever saw with her nose pierced. Too cool. I wanted to do it. Didn't have the guts. Or maybe I was just afraid of social criticism. Whatever. Time passes. Decades.

I'm ready to do it but it was a long time before there was a decent piercing parlour in downtown Fondis. Decades, maybe. You can't just go anywhere. You gotta check the place out, make sure it's clean, follows state guidelines. Make sure you're safe. The new place in Fondis qualified.

I had the place and I had the moon calendar. Made an appointment in the dark of the moon and thumbed a ride over.

"Did it hurt?" many ask.

Duh. Most people who ask have had their ears pierced, a much more painful and annoying procedure. I've had more pain from clueless nurses jabbing me in the arm with a needle.

What surprises me more than that question is how many women want to get a nose piercing. And how many already have their noses pierced. Or eyebrows. Or belly buttons. Or...

Life is about decoration and the body is an excellent canvas. Pain is temporary and an initiation.

The goddess smiles on us as we make our choices.

Some squeal and retreat. Others smile.

I smile.

XXIV.

BUILDING ON OUR DIFFERENCES

Epona Maris

I am no expert on the differences between men and women, but I do know that they make building a house more difficult. I was young, independent and had idealistic dreams of a rustic log cabin in the woods. Jerry was a bit older, more seasoned, and knew the value of indoor plumbing from direct experience on worksites. From the way we argued over plans, you would think we were married.

When I decided that I would use most of the money I inherited from my parents to build a home in the hills above Fondis, I knew that Jerry was the man to hire. He had been two years ahead of me at West Bijou High, but he went right to work after graduation, first in his father's construction company, then on his own.

He specialized in custom homes despite an antipathy to what he called "behemoths of the deep," those 5000 square foot palaces that are built as much for show as for living in. I was sure that he would love my romantic dreams of a tiny cabin with a woodstove for heat, kerosene lanterns and a pump for water in the yard.

"That'll be crap for resale value," he told me as he studied my pile of sketches.

"I don't care," I told him, "since I plan to live there the rest of my life."

He stared at me for a moment, then shrugged. "How do you plan to get it past the code inspector?"

I hadn't thought of that. "OK, you can wire it and plumb it and I just won't use it."

"Suit yourself," he said, flipping through the sketches again. "You need a bigger kitchen."

"Why? It will just be me living there."

He shrugged again. "You never know. This kitchen's too small for a fridge to open."

"But I won't have a fridge," I insisted. My voice was starting to get a bit sharp.

"It doesn't make sense to have that many windows," he said, as if he didn't hear my tone.

"I want them," I nearly spit through my teeth. "I want to look out of them."

"Uh-huh," he said, non-commitally. "We need to add a porch and mudroom."

"This is my house, I'm going to live there, not you. I'm just paying you to build the damn thing," I shouted at him.

"No—you're contracting for my expertise. You're getting it," he said, his voice a bit sharp, too. "And don't you think of hiring someone else who will tuck their tail and do whatever you tell him. You'll get crap." With that, he took the sketches and left. He broke ground for my cabin a month later while the summer grass grew long in the meadow.

The porch and mudroom turned out to be wonderful. The carved trim he added around the woodstove is beautiful, even though he didn't tell me before he did it. Now that I'm a little older, I even decided that electric light is better for writing under and an indoor toilet is a lot more sensible in the winter. But I got all of my windows, even though I did have to take a chainsaw to a couple of walls to get him to install them. Somehow, we're still friends.

XXV.

LUGHNASA FESTIVITIES

Deirdre H. Moon

I wandered into THE Art Gallery on a side street in Fondis (THE stands for "Theatrical Hysterical Experience.") The polished hardwood floors shone and the walls disappeared with an abundance of paintings. Sculptures rose mounted on cubes. Refreshment tables stood in front of the curtained stage at the far end. Faeries skitter about, whirling and laughing and pointing with delight at different artistic creations.

Most summer weekdays find the space filled with children learning theatre arts and other creative expression. THE volunteers transform the space from gallery to theatre with a minimum of effort. Many hands and much laughter get the work done efficiently.

This night THE Art Gallery is celebrating Lughnassa and everyone is dressed in sun symbols. The children will put on a play about the Celtic origins of the holiday. I'm wearing gold lamé harem pants and a shimmering gold sequin blouse over a gold leotard. I mean, it is a costume party. I always worry about that when I am invited to dress up. What if I'm the only one? Well, not much chance of that at THE. The little office behind the stage is filled with scrapbooks of THE events, all filled with outrageous costumed revelers.

After perusing the artwork, I cruise the crowd, listening, okay, eavesdropping. Some people discuss local politics but the comments are standard and each person is set on his or her candidate. The August primary will indicate who will win in November. While Fondis may have a spectrum of political beliefs, the county is tipped heavily to the Republican majority who always nab the local ticket in the general election. Primary pandemonium bubbles.

I grinned at the gnome balanced precariously on the rafters, furiously taking notes. They have their own newspaper, you know.

The mayor makes his rounds, accompanied by his simpering wife. He's in his cups. She isn't. Neither of them looks at the art. They're looking for votes.

Discussions become more heated as national politics takes the lead. Many have seen *Fahrenheit 9/11*; others have read Al Franken's *Lies and the Lying Liars Who Tell Them* Or *House of Bush, House of Saud*. One mentioned *The Essential America: Our Founders & The Liberal Tradition* by Senator George McGovern, former presidential candidate. There is not a faerie in sight—they scattered as the humans heated up.

Fear rides behind the anger, concern for the troops, sadness at the death of over 1000 in Iraq, fear of the loss of personal freedoms, fear of fascism, fear of helplessness, fear that once again the populous vote will be discounted.

"Abolish the electoral college." "We invaded the wrong country." "This is a high stakes election." "We had a balanced budget. Now, there's out of control government spending." "Republicans are no longer fiscally responsible." "Seventy five percent of the voters are disenfranchised." "My vote doesn't count."

Boomerang Blake Spicer claps his hands and calls the crowd to attention as the curtains are pulled. The political debaters clamp their lips and turn toward the stage. Spicer introduces the Fondis Players. After the play, a standing ovation. I tidy up tables, throw out paper plates, plastic cups. And then slip through the crowd to make a quick exit into the night under a waning moon.

Election. Mercury retrograde. It may all seem madness. The faeries tug at my golden wrap and giggle. "Don't take it too seriously."

"It'll all come out in the wash," my grandmother used to say. These guys are all bleached out. No red, white and blue left. Whatever will come out in the wash?

"It's all for the best," the Quiet Queen will murmur when I talk to her later. I want to believe her. But she has a Scorpio ascendant and isn't saying all she knows.

XXVI.

OBSTACLE COURSES

Roger Rural

OBSTACLE: (*n*) 1. The name of your great-aunt's brother-in-law; 2. The name of a new minivan; 3. Something that requires surgical removal; 4. A prominent and sometimes permanent hazard.

On typing paper, taped to the window next to the door going to the backyard are two drawings of the same rabbit: one, by my daughter and the other, by my spouse, which they put up as a memorial.

Year in, year out, the springtime refrain is the same: "Have you fed the turkeys? Have you fed the goats? Have you fed the chickens? Does everyone have water?" and the inevitable chorus comes after: "Daddy! On a commercial!"

In the backyard, just where some unsuspecting father can step while trying to chase a goose or an errant turkey, is a series of tires, a ladder, a bunch of bricks, a board, and a rope hung threateningly from the branches of a small peach tree. The children call it an obstacle course. They are quite proud of it. One walks on the rungs of the ladder, plays hopscotch on the tires, then ambles on the bricks, balances on a 2x4, then swings from the rope into the trunk of the tree.

My son, Raul, assures me that mastering this course will be useful in later life, when one doesn't have the advantages of thinking things through, but just needs to perform noble acts. Since I am of the age where I perform noble acts on a daily basis without benefit of an obstacle course or thinking things through, I marvel at his forethought every time I slip on the marbles he and his sister have left on the garage floor or trip over the bicycles on the driveway in the half dark of dawn when I am trying to feed the pigs before I go to work, where I perform noble acts.

"When I was Raul's age, I didn't want my little brother along," I marveled to Mrs. Rural. "But Raul and Rachel, even though he's eleven and she's five, do all sorts of things together!" *Most of them to kill their father, I thought.*

"When you were his age," she replied, "You probably had some playmates from your neighborhood. "He doesn't; so he cultivates his sister like a rare plant. It's a shame you didn't do that with your brother."

I agree silently and think of the obstacle course that was my brother, who, at age thirty-one, couldn't do his own laundry because his sickness made him weak. I washed, dried, bleached, and folded his laundry. Then I put it away. The obstacle course that he was disappeared and we enjoyed simple meals together and shared what we had loved and disliked of our parents. He died three months later.

There's a tremendous responsibility to taking care of animals: an unwritten contract that they'll be fed, watered, and allowed to eat nothing that will harm them; they'll be sheltered in winter and cooled in summer; they'll have clean pens and stalls and coops. They will be safe. Hearing children slough it off to watch a cartoon or a show about incompetent adults is painful to me, and I think of my father in law, who made his daughters take care of their horses before watching re-runs of *StarTrek*: perhaps his uncompromising attitude is one I should take.

It's six o'clock and my son proudly announces that everyone has been fed and watered and taken care of for another day. He and his sister have distributed the feed, gathered the eggs, watered all the animals, and have left none. He is especially proud because he carries in his heart the obstacle of his sister's bunny, the one whose pictures adorn the window toward the backyard, whom he sat on, quite accidentally, and killed.

XXVII.

TO EACH HER OWN

Epona Maris

The cradle was to be a baby shower present for my friend Lucinda, who was due that summer. I had made it myself from Fondis pinewood and decorated it with Celtic knotwork. I filled it with a soft lilac quilt and placed it near the window, to admire it in the midsummer sun. Somehow, it felt wrong to leave it empty, so I placed my grandmother's porcelain-faced doll under the quilt, its blond curls spilling over it. Satisfied, I went about my chores for the day.

I woke just after midnight to shrieks like a cat trapped in a well. Despite realizing that the sound was coming from within my cabin, I don't think I was really awake by the time I tracked it to its source in the cradle. My grandmother's doll was shrieking at me. But if it was her doll, what happened to its curly blonde hair?

It was the baldness of the current cradle resident that finally got through the muzziness in my head. This was not a doll: it was a real baby. It was an odd baby, with long, drawn features, gray-tinted skin and little pointy teeth that I could easily see when it opened its mouth to shriek, which it did often. I was totally at a loss for what to do.

I didn't think that Lucinda would like to receive her present complete with a shrieking strange child. I didn't know anything about raising babies—I had barely figured out puppies so far. I needed an expert.

"What do I do with a shrieking baby?" I asked my friend Dorothy over the phone. She was a caseworker for Social Services, so I figured she would know.

"What?" she asked, clearly waking up as slowly as I had.

"Shrieking baby. Can't you hear it?"

"When did you have a baby?" she reasonably asked.

"I found it tonight," I answered, just as reasonably.

"You found it? I'm coming right over." As she hung up, I realized that I still had the same problem: the shrieks had not lessened.

"Milk," I said to it. "Babies like milk." It quieted a little when I picked it up and carted it to the goat barn. I got a doe onto the milking stand and held the baby under it.

When the mouth opened for the next shriek, I stuck a teat in. Maybe it was just surprised, but it shut up for the moment and sucked.

"You can't just feed a baby straight form a goat," Dorothy said when she arrived.

"Why not?" I asked, since it obviously was working.

"It isn't sanitary."

"Oh," I said. I had forgotten that babies need things really clean. At least that's how I had always seen them handled. I pulled the teat out of its mouth. The shrieking resumed, but a little less enthusiastically.

"We have to find its mother," Dorothy said. "It's against the law to just drop your baby off at a stranger's house."

"Oh," I said again. I hadn't thought of that, either. As I looked at the baby I held in my arms, it suddenly opened its eyes and looked back at me. The pupils were slitted like a cat's. "I don't think its mother cares much about our laws," I told Dorothy. "Her folks have been dropping off changelings for centuries."

Dorothy just stared at me as if I had said something nuts. Before she could think of a suitable remark, however, the baby's mother appeared behind her in the doorway, holding my grandmother's doll. The faerie woman was slender and ethereal as most were, but her brindle hair was short cropped around her pointed ears. She held the doll out to me: "I choose not to hold to our trade," she said. "This child of yours is far too quiet."

I traded faerie child for porcelain doll without hesitation. As the mother carried her shrieking burden into the dark, Dorothy caught at her silk sleeve. "Wait, you can't just walk off with that baby before I determine if you can raise it safely!"

The faerie didn't even comment as she faded into the night.

XXVIII.

WHALE CALL

Deirdre H. Moon

Sweat trickles between my breasts. I wipe my forehead with the back of my hand and signal to Arianrhod that we should take a break. She's been helping me in the garden and the weeds still seem to be winning the battle.

I pour electrolytes from a thermos, hand Arianrhod a cup and we scoot down on the garden path, seeking shade beneath a towering catnip. I toss down the liquid and stretch out, watching a few puffy clouds that I hope will invite afternoon rain.

"It was crowded in downtown Fondis when I drove through." She's sipping her libation.

"Raging Republican Reggie called last night. She's all agog because the President is coming for the big Fondis Fourth of July parade." I shrug. "Big deal. Security everywhere. Local folks can't use Fondis International Airport. It's a good time for me to stay here at the yurt and avoid the crowds. Thanks again for helping me in the garden."

She smiles and turns to communicate with the devas of the sunflowers. All the flowers are glorious with last month's rain.

My cell phone vibrates in the pocket of my overalls. "Caterpillar," I answer. It's my latest whimsy. Answering with a nonsensical word. I collect words. Broccoli. Platypus. Fiddle-faddle.

"Oh, hi, Cerridwen." Perhaps I should be more formal with the old wise woman. But she chuckles. I listen. Nod. Frown and disconnect.

Arianrhod is running her hands over the aura of the roses. I hate to interrupt.

"I need to go see Cerridwen. Sort of a command performance. I am requested to go now."

Arianrhod finishes her blessing and turns. "Okay." She is so amenable. "Would you like me to give you a ride across the valley? Maybe you know some shortcuts to avoid all that traffic." Indeed I do.

Later I sit under the pyramid with Cerridwen, listening, trying to keep my mouth closed, trying not to protest.

"So, let me get this straight. The dream I had last night was a message you were to give me today?" She smiles. Her white hair glows.

Whales came to me, circled me and I dove deep into the ocean and surfaced. They sang to me, a sweet and sometimes mournful song, calling me, luring me.

"I am to leave Fondis? Actually, in real time, follow the voice of the whales?" She nods, oblivious to my concern.

"What about the yurt? What about my place on the wheel to ground the energy here? What...?"

"Another will take your place while you are gone. Nothing is forever. Go. Walk the beaches. Swim the ocean. Listen. And return with their wisdom."

It is my turn to nod. Befuddled.

She hands me an airline ticket and slips a scrimshaw necklace around my neck. The image: a whale.

"Trust. You will be guided."

I don't know when I'll be back in Fondis. This feels abrupt. But I will do my best to trust. To follow the adventure. To know that Spirit guides me. To the whales.

XXIX.

TAKING SHORTCUTS

Roger Rural

Shortcut: *(n, v)* 1. A particular type of haircut; 2. Something Procrustes was fond of in tall people; 3. A quicker way that doesn't take much time, sometimes becoming meaningless, as in "A quicker college, faster."

"I never want you to think a shortcut is good enough," I hissed at my son, "and I want you to appreciate what's going on here." We were in the Poultry Barn at 3:30 on Thursday afternoon, awaiting Raul's showmanship interview, and the judge, who had begun his work at 8:00 that morning, was still not done. He'd finished Guinea Fowl and was beginning to examine eggs.

"Eggs?" Raul asked incredulously, "Eggs?"

I think my son is on this earth to teach me patience. "He's examining them for thickness; strength; marketability; consistency, Raul: That's important."

"An egg's an egg," he grumbled. "What's important is that we shoulda' been outta' here five hours ago."

I smiled, thinking of patience. "Don't you think he should truly assess the birds all you 4-Hers have raised? Don't you think he should spend time doing that?"

"No. I want an award and I want to go home."

"You really want him to take a shortcut, and not honor all the fine work you've put in?"

"Yeah," he said petulantly. "Hang an award on a chicken and go home."

"And if it's the wrong chicken?"

Raul shrugged.

"No, Raul; when you thought about it, you'd regret his doing that. What use would it be to raise a decent turkey if he did that?"

"They've done it in other barns," he observed.

"Yeah; and remember what happened to the contestant? Remember that Sharlee was so irritated with that guy in the Pig Barn that she never showed again? Remember when Jordan got last place for his goat? They both left 4-H and they both stopped raising animals because the judges took shortcuts. You'd probably stop raising turkeys if the judge didn't show some care."

"It'd be easier," he replied.

"But it would haunt you forever."

My dad, an attorney for 35 years, never actually sat for his Bar Examination: In Colorado, veterans of World War II, finishing law school in 1947, were immediately issued their licenses by an overly grateful legislature, which saw their sacrifices as worth their licenses. My father, therefore, never knew if he were truly qualified to practice law in Colorado, and I believe that shortcut haunted him throughout his career, keeping him from the success that a well-connected young man of those times could enjoy. His younger brother, who was also a veteran, enrolled in law school after the waiver had ceased, and had to sit for the Bar Examination. His younger brother was rich and successful.

When the turkey poults arrive from the feed store, we hike up the thermostat in a basement room to 90 degrees Farenheit and keep a light shining on their cage to help keep them warm. There is no shortcut. We cover the cage in old blankets to keep drafts out. Those little birds become an obsession. Finally, after some die, those who have survived their first four weeks are moved outside, to a pen, where still a couple more die; maybe a couple more, because of predators, also die. It's a dreary, sad and uncompromising business.

"Think about the time you spent, Raul. Think about the wintry winters and the blooming springs and tell me if that judge shouldn't look at your work and judge it against everybody else's to determine the best against the very best in the nation."

"But it takes so long!" he groaned.

"Yeah. And in that length of time, imagine yourself in his shoes, wanting to do a good job. He probably once had turkeys that moulted, like yours did, just at the wrong time, and he probably fed them protein, just like you did, to make a fine looking bird. What's important is to take the experience and learn from it: Don't take the shortcut. Don't take the easy way out. You won't grow."

He had that look on his face: half boredom, half rage, that I imagine his Math teacher found endearing as he earned his C at semester last year; and I knew he didn't want to hear it, so I continued: "Look at our friend Maria,

Raul: She's voted for the majority party in this county for as long as there's been dirt; but she's realized, recently, that the current commissioners have taken a bunch of shortcuts, and the County's in financial trouble. She wants a clean county. She doesn't want shortcuts. She's probably going to vote for the minority party because they won't take shortcuts."

Raul's turkey won third because of a smaller breast than the two who preceded it, and Raul won eleventh in showmanship at 5:00 that afternoon. There were eleven candidates in showmanship: Contestants telling the judge about turkeys: their care, feeding, breeding, size, and so on.

"He asked the wrong questions," Raul observed as I pulled the car out of the parking lot.

"No. You depended on shortcuts in your answers," I replied.

He was quiet during the long drive home to Fondis.

XXX.

FALLING OFF THE WAGON FOREVER

Epona Maris

Autumn is the season of change for me. Spring may dance to the tune of fresh new life, summer may ripen the harmonies and winter silence them, but fall is the turning point, the bridge that lifts the melody into patterns unheard by even the composer when the song began.

It was the autumn of my senior year of college when I completed a circle. I had begun my freshman year as an English major, full of dreams of becoming a best-selling writer. By my sophomore year, my parents' message of pragmatism had sunk in: I needed to find a career that would provide a steady job. Few writers are ever good enough to make much money. My parents worried about my future. To be fair to them, they were paying the bill for my flights of fancy.

I quickly rejected business courses as beyond my ability to tolerate. Physics was interesting, but I could not see myself in a lab coat and real shoes. Teaching was out, regardless of the subject, because I had spent too many years desperately trying to get out of school. I turned to Psychology in order to figure myself out, more than any other reason.

Psychology classes led to internships. Watching (and occasionally participating) in the Friday night sport of beer guzzling led to an interest in substance abuse counseling. Putting the two together led to my summer job at a nearby detoxification facility. That led to a true understanding of my place in the world.

Joe Flannery was a weekend regular at the detox. After years of practice, he had reached the prestigious achievement of a Blood Alcohol Content of .5 on more occasions than any other of the frequent flyers. He was also, being Irish, a poet.

"Down by the salley gardens my love and I did meet," he proclaimed, with liquored breath, the first time we met. "She passed the salley gardens with little snow-white feet," he added, following me down the hall as I checked beds. "She bid me take love easy, as the leaves grow on the tree," he was putting heart and soul into it by this point, swinging his arms wide, as I quickened my steps. "But I, being young and foolish, with her would not agree," he ended, bouncing against the wall. I ran for the shelter of the nursing station, with W. B. Yeats rolling about in my brain.

"Let me go free, love," Joe said to me at the end of my shift, when he was nearing the first hint of sobriety. His eyes danced as he smiled his most charming smile. "My heart yearns for the open hills." I knew that his heart was really just yearning for another drink, but he was on an Emergency Commitment, so he was locked behind the detox door. Denied freedom, he slumped back onto the common room couch and stared at the sitcom on tv. The keys weighed heavy in my pocket as I went back to documenting vital signs.

As I opened the door to leave, I heard "Excuse me, love," behind me, then Joe slipped past. I opened my mouth to call the rest of the staff, but stayed silent, watching him dance into the night.

"Welcome, O life!" Joe declaimed, arms spread wide. "I go to encounter for the millionth time the reality of experience and to forge in the smithy of my soul the uncreated conscience of my race."

James Joyce, my unconscious mind commented. *A Portrait of the Artist as a Young Man.* Suddenly, the doors of my mental literature class flung wide open. "Old father, old artificer," I answered him, "stand me now and ever in good stead." He waved graciously, then disappeared.

I quit my job at the detox that evening, then went to the college office to change my major. I gave in to the temptations of poetry to the point of intoxication and refuse to ever become sober again.

I suppose I could have talked my way back into the job at the detox, given how hard it is for them to keep employees, but I knew I was lost to that work. I have no right to hold the keys.

XXXI.

UNDERWATER

Deirdre H. Moon

Neptune confiscated my cell phone upon arrival. Said it interfered with the energetic process of non-verbal transmission. Plus it violated the lower oceanic realms where I was to reside.

Serena the Selkie returned to the watery depths as my teacher. I spent a year contemplating a sand dollar. The depths of that truth cannot here be told.

I walked the labyrinth on the ocean's floor, so deep and dark that only rare shafts of glittering light penetrate to these depths. My right and left brains not only bridged but merged.

Sirian Lightbeings triangled my sleep patterns, altering my DNA. A triangle in a spiral, too weird to describe. Dream and reality flip flopped—or coincided. I am not confused, just luxuriating in the cool wonder of the briny deep, so far removed from the hustle and bustle of Fondis.

Now I float, forgetful of the fast track back home. Merlina the Mermaid glides into view. Water faeries whisper into strands of my hair streaming out like seaweed.

Merlina sings a message to me. While friends and family are sweltering in Fondis, I am luxuriating in the calm, cool depths. Merlina asks if I want to go back.

"Not yet." We don't really talk to each other. We think to each other. She sings. I know what she is saying as she knows also my thoughts. Perhaps on a tour of our nation's capitol, that might be an intimidating way to communicate. Imagine all the politicians really know what each other think. Whooeee.

I must be getting vibes from above. I don't usually think about things like that at all down here. I suppose I will all too soon get the call from Cerridwen that it is time to return.

Merlina lets me know that She Who Knows All is also headed for the shore but not deep down beneath the ocean waves. Her journey will have its own calling.

The Lady of the Lake has just returned from the Green Isle. Each person drawn to and guided to the right place at the right time.

Enjoy your summer wherever you are.

Autumn

FAITH, DOUBT AND JOY

Epona Maris

Three things that turn me
Through the spirals of my life:
Faith, Doubt and Joy.

Faith flies on wings of thistle-down;
It is a mystery how the wind
Holds her in the sky.
It is not of her own accord that she moves
Through the realm of spirit to touch flesh.
She is drawn to the flame
That burns lesser dreams to ash.
She passes through the fire, refined.
Her eyes are stars shining
For me to follow when I clear my mind to see.

Faith floats into my heart,
Growing roots to the ground, branches to the sky,
Flowing water through my thirsting soul,
Transforming the core of me
Into shining light.
"Time has no meaning," she tells me,
"The journey is all."

I believe.
I believe my words have meaning.
I believe they flow through me for me to share
With others who hear the call of wild birds on the wind,
Wishing for wings to fly.

On faith, I start writing this poem, trusting
That the words will hit against each other hard enough
To spark song.
I have faith despite the bitter lessons taught by life.
I have faith that I am on the path,
Faith in the process,
But I doubt the timing and my own thoughts.

Doubt is a tether, tying thoughts to deeds
In patterns that reflect my fears.
She wakes me in the silence of the night
Reminding me of words spoken,
Actions not done, meanings uncertain.
She wakes in me a bone-deep longing for truth.

Doubt is a taskmaster, teaching me the grounded pattern
Of late-night reflections,
The value of persistence despite pain.
"Dreams are worth nothing in the marketplace,"
      she tells me,
"just a scattering of loose feelings, drifting nowhere."
And "The world is full of misspent dreamers."
I dream anyway, dream of spinning straw to gold,
Dry words into forests of verse
That welcome eager wanderers home.

Searching, I stare blindly at lines on paper.
"Sharpen those words long enough and they'll cut you
      through the heart."
I falter, hearing her drone surround me:
"Not good enough, not good enough, not enough,
Never enough."
I run, hide, wish the world away.
I think I am alone, lost in the monotony of daily tasks,
But doubt finds me.
She follows my footsteps, deep as a toad croaking:
"Remember, remember, try to remember
Before it is too late."

I do my best to remember what I should,
Remember what I should be.
Despite the respectable face I learn to face the world with,
The words find me, fill me, flow through my fingers.
But then the words shatter at my touch,
Fall like dead flies scattered on a frost-touched window sill.
I find myself asking "Why?" with no answer
Except: "No reason."
It all makes no sense.
I hold myself silent as doubt runs its course through me,
Draining my mind, my thoughts dripping slow like honey
Down the sides of a jar,
Pooling in the depths of me.

When it is done, I breathe deep,
Turn again to try again.

And so I dance the spiral patterns, trading partners:
First Faith holds out her hand to me, then Doubt
        draws me near.
Both follow familiar rhythms, despite my faltering steps.
I forget where I lead, where I follow,
Where I am.

Joy brings me back to my senses,
Back to the touch, smell, sound, taste, sight of life
        in the moment.
Joy lies hidden within
The small things in life:
The turn of a bird's wings in the summer sun,
The feel of feathers soft on skin,
Unexpected moments.
She shelters within the spiral shell, just beyond sight,
Hiding when I turn to look for her,
Then slipping out to surprise me,
Starlight on the shadow edge of thought.

Joy is a child with swan feathers sheltering a candle flame.
She does not speak to me, only smiles,
Weaving her fingers through the fire,
Coaxing the air to sing.
I want to hold her to my heart, but she slips away,
Then tiptoes up to me when I least expect her.

Joy brings laughter and light to the pattern of my dance,
She renews my faith in who I am, faith in the world
That holds mysteries within each hidden corner.
Joy laughs with me at Doubt, reminds me that the blade
Cuts whichever way I choose.
Joy brings the rhythmic music for my feet to follow,
Drumbeats and crystal chimes, trills of harp strings.
And so I dance:
Turning in the spiral of faith, doubt and joy, I am.

I am the thistle-down of thoughts unspoken,
I am the wind that lifts wings to flight.
I am the flame that draws metal from stone,
Refined into stars of light.

I am roots and branches, earth and sky,
Filled with the flow of shining water.
I am the journey that takes no time,
Travels no distance, that never ends.

I am the wild bird on the wind's wing,
The spark of song that sweetens
Life's bitter edge:
I walk the poet's path.

I walk the silent patterns of the night
That tell of truth.
I spin straw to gold, words into forests.
I hold open the welcoming door.

I am the spiral shell,
The swan feathers that shelter the candle flame,
I am the woven air of song.

I am the mystery of the world,
The blade of choice,
The drumbeat and the harp string
That pattern the spiral dance.

    Of everything, I am.

XXXII.

MERMAID 101

Deirdre H. Moon

Mermaid 101 isn't as easy as it might sound.

In truth, this is my third try at it. If I don't "get it" this time, I'll probably have to go to Remedial Mermaid Training. How humiliating.

I'll just have to try harder. When Neptune dropped by to observe one day, he said that was my problem. I was trying too hard.

"Let it go. Visualize the fin. Feel the movement. Then let it go," his deep roar rumbled bubbles through the ocean depths.

Once again I close my eyes, shift my focus, feel the sweet salt water caress my body, feel my legs merging into a rainbow colored tail. Yes. I've almost got it. I open my eyes, see pixilated dabs of color scintillating into almost form.

I flex my muscles and shoot out of the cove where I've been practicing. Without effort I'm suddenly in the middle of a dance of dolphins. Oh, wow. This is fabulous. I wonder where Neptune is now? I can't wait to show him.

With that thought, I plummet to the ocean floor. Two legs walking. One of the great truths of learning and I seem to forget it.

Merlina glides toward me with a smile. She is my mermaid role model and I think she just saw me fail. Again. I drop my chin not wanting to meet her eyes.

"Deirdre, you did it! Now all it will take is a little more practice." We don't really talk. I just hear her thoughts in my head. I glance up. She means it. I start to feel better.

"Thank you." I nod to her in gratitude.

"I regret interrupting your practice session. However, the Ocean Goddess wishes your presence. Now." She glows as the message is delivered.

"The Ocean Goddess? I thought Neptune was in charge down here," I stutter, confused and pleased that there is the representation of the divine feminine at the depths of our beloved planet.

"He thinks he is." She giggles.

Mermaid giggles tickle my ear like faerie whispers.

"For the time, you will refer to her as Oceana. Perhaps later she will share more with you. Now, I will rest, while you re-form your mermaid tail and I will guide you to her." Her image pixilates, fuzzes and she closes her eyes, resting in her auric field.

She is there without judgment, trusting me. I feel safe and in the blink of an underwater eye, I am in mermaid form. As I glance up from my shimmering beautiful tail, she is beside me and we swim in places I've never imagined, into deep ravines, past towering forests of seaweed, amidst a grand diversity of underwater life and into a cave. Deep into the cave, dark, winding corridors glinting, shining, guiding me down deeper.

I burst into a huge cavern of blasting light, golden and glorious. Merlina is no longer with me. The Ocean Goddess forms lightly in the heart of the cave, her essence shining almost beyond the scope of my eyes.

"Deirdre, you have far exceeded our expectations of your visit here. We love your energy and regret your departure."

"My departure?" A great sadness is already tugging at my heart, constricting my throat. "No."

"Fondis needs you now. You will return here again in time and remember all that you have learned. For now you must return Earthside and be of service."

She embraces me and I fall into her heart, feel her love and compassion and know we are traveling beyond the moment.

I awaken in my bed in the yurt on the ledge above Fondis and close my eyes. Re-entry will take its time.

XXXIII.

SUBTERRANEAN ADVENTURES

Roger Rural

Subterranean: (adj) 1. Having to do with under the surface of the earth; 2. Not the regular teacher in homeroom; 3. The name of a car that did not sell very well.

On the walls in many home study areas or home offices, people proudly display their degrees from places of higher learning, their licenses, and a few congratulatory items, such as plaques, ribbons, trophies, and certificates. These certificates, more than anything else, indicate what the owner of the property considers worth remembering.

I have never, however, seen displayed the one we all get when we buy a house in a rural area: That which certifies the septic system is in good working order. The degree from Oxford, the Ph.D. from the University of Colorado, the Coach of A Lifetime plaque pale in importance; especially when the septic system doesn't work properly, usually when it's least expected, like on Thanksgiving.

There is some disagreement among archaeologists and historians over why so many of the settlers died at Plymouth, Massachusetts, in the winter of 1620-1621. We know them as the Pilgrims, or the Puritans, who fled religious persecution in England and Holland and finally found a home in the New World, where they could worship as they pleased. When half of their number died, their chroniclers attributed it to starvation. Some archaeologists and historians attribute it to bad sanitation because they built their outhouses too close to their water source.

It's strange, really: an archaeologist, when digging up Macchu Picchu, Rome, or any other ancient site, will aim for the dump and the septic system first because what is thrown away is usually more valuable to understanding daily life than what is preserved.

And what an archaeologist knows is that she can study the septic system and determine the sophistication of the culture and its technical savvy. Was it cobbled together from spare parts or was it manufactured for the purpose it served? It's surprising to think that our systems are no different, really, from that of some Romans, who also understood sending waste into the ground via pipes and propelled by water. The main difference we have in the Twenty First Century is the septic tank, which breaks down waste and then sends it to a leeching field: a series of perforated pipes buried underground and surrounded by small rocks. The water and waste trickle through these into the earth.

When we bought our house, I got a telephone call from the woman whose husband cleaned our septic tank:

"If you put anything like cigarette butts or tampons or paper that's got perfumes or dyes and not made for it down the toilet, you will be sorry," she warned, in a voice like that of a Puritan.

I answered solemnly that I would not do anything wrong ever again with my toilet. I have not erred from that because I have been afraid that she might call me again.

One of the reasons for the first Thanksgiving, I believe, is because the settlers at Plymouth learned a great deal more than agriculture from the Native Americans: I believe they learned how to keep their outhouses well away from their water source. They were city people, after all, and hadn't much idea as to where their food came from or how to insure clean water. That was someone else's job in the cities of the Netherlands and in England.

"Your water source, the wellhead, is at least half an acre away from your leeching field," the Puritan septic lady told me. *"Make sure you keep it that way."* I solemnly promised I would not move my well.

"Good," she said. *"Move it and you'll be sorry."*

We have no need to move it. We probably never will move it.

The Puritans, on the other hand, needed to move their waste from their drinking water. Sketches of the colony in summer, 1621, show a bunch of houses well away from the water supply. Unfortunately, there is no literature about it. Prayers and religious meditations from that time seem to have excluded it completely; very like the septic system certificate of today: known; but not spoken about.

But perhaps, when some archaeologist or scholar studies Puritan life, she will find some little homily or rhyme dedicated to septic systems. After all, these were people who reminded themselves daily of who they were and what their goals were, for instance:

"In Adam's fall, *and: "Think thou, on sin*
We sinned all." *And never let it touch*
  your skin,"

And: *"An idle mind is the Devil's workshop."*

So I can imagine the Puritan, cheerfully building a home at Plymouth in the summer of 1621, reciting:
"Keep your outhouse well away
From the water you have drunk this day."

XXXIV.

CHOICES AND CHANGES

Epona Maris

Choice and change: both are inevitable and both illusory. The first crisp mornings of September cause me to muse about choice and change, much like any budding Freshman gathering up belongings for her first days at college. What to take, what to leave behind, what is to come? When I was faced with those choices and changes, I thought I was eager for them until the time came to prove it.

I had completed all of the requisite classes, tests, essays and forms, so I was scheduled to attend a university out of state (there was no college in Fondis at that time). Since I liked to write I decided on an English major, but hadn't thought much beyond that declaration.

My father said: "Make sure you take a bookkeeping course so you have a skill that will support you." Since I was arguing with everyone then, I had to argue with him, until my mother told me to get out of the house and "walk off that sour mood." I took to the hills, as usual. I have always liked to wander in the trees, but that fall it had become an obsession for me to find the faerie mound again. The one I had tripped over on a full-moon summer night, leading to the curse that I could never pass by an argument but must always argue for the less well-defended side.

Somehow, that seemed to mean that I was arguing with everyone at anytime. I was angry, irritated and more than a little confused by it (especially after losing a college scholarship when the mayor of Fondis said I was the most deserving candidate, leading me to argue for my competition). I wanted an explanation, I wanted to learn how to manage this affliction, but, more than that, I wanted to find the magic again.

The magic, apparently, did not want to be found. I walked in the forest each evening, trying to recapture the abstracted frame of mind that had led me between worlds that night, but my mind would not cooperate. I turned at every faint movement, hoping to see the sharp-pricked ears of a fox or the red brush of tail, but I was alone.

I determined that I needed advice, so I went looking for the one person with a weirder reputation than mine. I found Deirdre Moon in the teahouse on Main Street, sipping Oolong and knitting a sock. She looked up at me calmly as I spilled a rambling tale of fox faeries and wandering geese. Shifting from foot to foot in front of her tea table, I railed against my argumentation curse, then found myself arguing against my resentment of it.

When I finally ran down to silence, she looked as if she would speak. I tensed, waiting for her to make a statement that I would have to argue against. Instead, she knitted a row, then asked: "What will it take for you to believe in yourself?" I found myself with nothing to respond. She handed me a book with a triple spiral on its leather cover, then went back to her knitting. I opened the book to find that it was blank except for one line: "When given two choices, always take the third."

The next evening, as the sun set and the full moon rose, I went to say goodbye to Hissy and Esmeralda in the goose yard. All three of us looked up to watch a V of wild geese flying west over our heads. I heard a yipping and looked down to see a fox dancing in the field. I laughed as she chased her tail then leaped high into the air after the flying geese. She turned to look at me, laughing too, then disappeared into the forest.

The next morning, I packed the last few items I would take with me to college: two goose feather quill pens, a cord tied with fox hairs, and a nearly-blank book. The magic chose to follow of its own accord.

XXXV.

DREAMS AND NIGHTMARES

Deirdre H. Moon

I stick out my thumb, hoping to catch a ride on the four-lane fastway. Crunching gravel spins across lanes, bites my ankles. A long black hearse with polished, darkened windows floats along on red balloon tires. It stops but I can't get in because the eagle flies above.

I sit up, wide awake, thanking the Great Goddess for real time, not nightmare illusions.

"Where'd all that come from?" I ask aloud.

She snickers. "Can a faerie fly for president?" She murmurs. I roll over, snuggle into the warm fur of Merlin, fat cat, and wish for a bowl of guacamole. My eyes slip to half mast, out of focus. An angel sits on the footboard of my bed. Her smile is gentle, reassuring, as her wings open to encompass me. Merlin purrs. In the distance, coyotes howl.

Death nudges a boney elbow into the angel's wing. She scowls. With a light breath, she blows him into a crumpled heap of bones on the floor. I'm having a bad Mercury retrograde time. I turn on the light and don't even see the faeries that usually dance upon the light rays.

I flip the pages of the calendar, counting the days to equinox. Equal daylight, equal night. I need some equality in my life. Soon, we shall have the reminder of balance, nature will supersede nightmares, leaves will fall and dance the trees toward the darkness of the year. Time, rhythm, cycles, birth, death, renewal.

I walk into the night air, listening to the frog song, the cricket chirp, the moan of moonlight. I am one with the Universe, free from self-imposed bonds and imagined fears, ready for the moment. Gabrielle, the Great Pyrenees, slides her head under my hand. I sit under the stars, contemplating my home planet and pet her velvet ears.

It's all good, as the Quiet Queen would say.

XXXVI.

RURAL ENTERTAINMENT

Roger Rural

"Early in the evening when the sun gets low
Pull out the fiddle and I rosin up the bow.
Kids are asleep so I keep it kinda' low,
Thank God I'm a country boy.
Well I got me a fine wife, I got me old fiddle;
When the sun's comin' up, I got cakes on the griddle.
Life ain't nothin' but a fuzzy wuzzy riddle—
Thank God I'm a country boy."
--John Denver, Aspen millionaire

YEAH, RIGHT!

Entertainment: *(n)* 1. Anything having to do with the bathtub at my house; 2. A form of suffering for the entertainer, usu. A clumsy adult; 3. Something on the television featuring the Attorney General.

    My friend Susan tells me that an introvert "creates worlds within worlds in his mind, and entertains himself that way, the same way a super trackster runs laps around a track; not only keeping fit but getting better." If so, I am vastly entertained.
    The vista of the Fondis Fire Protection District lies just below the horizon where I sit in my porch swing and watch the sunset with my four year-old daughter, imagining together buffalo coming over the hill two hundred years ago:
    "And there would've been hundreds of 'em, Rachel, all thundering over the hill—"
    "Is there a dinosaur there? And this house?"
    "I don't think so."
    "Daddy, can I watch a movie?"
    The vista of the Fondis Fire Protection District is a bit less distinct in the twilight as I return to the porch swing, hearing a bad Japanese video faintly from the living room behind me.
    Only about seventy five years ago, there was no radio out here; fifty years ago, limited television. Now there's an abundance of television and questionable taste on much of it. The newspaper, one hundred years ago, was one of the

sole means of entertainment; along with magazines and whoever stopped by from the metropolis of Hastings or Kutch.

"So what did kids do back then?" my son asked me, genuinely puzzled. Life without a television or VCR is incredibly hard for him to imagine, made harder by the fact that his viewing is restricted for failing to keep current on his homework.

They improvised, the same way he and his sister do now: a rope laid on the driveway becomes a raging torrent that the dinosaur cannot cross to get to its mommy on the other side unless the moose helps it; a bow and arrow is made from string and aspen branches; the inside of a brick is carefully examined after being beaten with Daddy's hammer on the garage floor; the cats who live in the garage are seen as a threat by the doll in a low chair "because they're going to steal her DNA."

Pretty smart cats.

I find, as I did once in high school when I weaned myself off of television, that I read more.

"Oh, there's no lack of opportunity here in the country," I was assured by a well-meaning septuagenarian when I first arrived. "Just come on down to the church; there's something everyday."

And she was right: I just did not want to do the somethings that were offered. I kind of missed museums that had multiple offerings and kind of missed a variety of styles and genres of live music and kind of missed fine dining and kind of missed convenience—that sort of thing.

But I find, and maybe it's because I have the leisure to consider what I have been entertained by, that a limited amount of entertainment is larger than anything I could have had in the city. Like the sunset, with its limited span, it's bigger, cheaper than Prozac, and it has more places for dinosaurs to play hide and seek.

XXXVII.

THE SENSE OF TIME

Epona Maris

    I have been accursed of having no sense of time. I do my best to meet the expectations of modern society by arriving and departing when the clock says the time is correct, but it takes little to distract me from that task. Friends know to schedule loosely when I am involved: 9:00 could mean 9:00, or it could mean 9:20 or 8:45. I am generally not rude enough to miss the mark by more than that amount, but I have never developed the skill to be consistently closer.

    But time is a multi-layered web, not easily described by slender hands that turn in circles, or numbers that progress to an orderly march beat. Time is as much in the mind as it is in the world at large, perhaps more so. Time can fly with the wind blowing across the ridge top or it can settle in the hot dust of the valley footpath, ready for an afternoon nap. I struggled to pattern time to my needs until I learned the secret of the travelling stone.

    I stumbled across the secret to time, literally, when I was wandering through the forest one early fall evening, just as the sun approached the hilltops. I knew there was an ancient stone marker in the area because the faeries had mentioned it, but I had never been able to find it. I was reminiscing about a pleasant evening I had recently had with friends in Ceridwen's moon grotto when the stone appeared in front of me through the gold-slanting last rays.

    Surprised, I tripped and nearly fell as my momentum carried me over it. I found myself in the moon grotto, wondering how I got there. As a voracious reader of fantasy stories, I knew quickly that I had found a means for instant travel. Making the technique work again proved to take a lot longer. I ended up walking back across the Bijou valley to get home near dawn. Even so, I was excited about my discovery.

    It took me three days of experimenting before I realized that the slower I approached the stone, the faster I found it. It took a few days longer to learn that the more I planned what I wanted it for, the longer it took to find it. Marking the spot did not help, since the stone was never quite in the same place twice. The stone refused to be used as a means to an end. On the other hand, if I was just curious about what was going on in town, or wondering who might be at Dierdre's medicine wheel, I could casually stroll right there.

I tried using the stone path when I am in a hurry to get somewhere, but it never appeared until after the time I needed to get there. It was a path with no purpose except to be traveled.

Time is what you make of it. Sometimes it is enough to just be in the moment.

XXXVIII.

A JOURNEY WEST

Deirdre H. Moon

"Do you want to visit the King of Cups?" Triscuit Suck Cheese asked through the static on her cell phone.

"Of course. But..." My thoughts jammed. "Tris, I'm not sure. It's a long way."

"We'll take the chariot," she reassured me.

"The beautiful cobalt blue chariot? Still we must pass through many kingdoms."

"Deirdre," she said it in that tone of voice that told me to get it together. "We will stop and explore. You can walk around. Take your staff for support. We can do it in three sunrises."

I am cautious about traveling companions. Tris and I haven't been on the road together for centuries. Will she tolerate my picky ways? Will I tolerate hers? Does it matter? The King of Cups is out there in the middle of the desert. Waiting.

I meet Tris in the crowded sprawl of the masses, a far distance from the peaceful ways of Fondis. Somehow Tris maneuvers past the dinosaurs and we head north while I gradually become aware of the morning unfolding from city to farmland to arid desert. I do not drink coffee so don't have the jump start on the day that Tris does.

We make a pit stop and go to a bathroom without a bath and no mirrors. Cross the border and carbo load on burritos and rice before we turn west. For entertainment we look for funky places, intending to send equally funky post cards. Buford is closed. At the next stop an old lady tells it burned last Tuesday.

Nab a photo op at a green highway sign that reads "open range." Beneath it is an old stove with the oven door open.

Get lost in the City of Salt. Guardian angels in a SUV speak to me in an unknown accent as I probe the map, asking directions. At last they shrug and indicate that they'll lead us back to I-80, the thoroughfare to the King's castle.

We stop at the Lake of Salt to taste it. Check out the funky faux copy of the Taj Mahal. The cell rings. It is Tris' son Fears No Heights. "Mom, it's lunch time. I'm hungry," he says in jest from a kingdom far away. After that the cell doesn't work. The cool blue chariot charges westward at close to legal speeds and comfortable temperatures.

Relentless, Tris guides Blue through endless desert, under blistering skies with no sign of habitation for hours. That's when she introduces me to her namesake. She produces a can of cheese. Really. A can. You press a button and it swirls out. I stick it in my mouth, laughing. She suggests a cracker. We push on through the desert light, munching these improbable snacks.

Two sunsets later we collapse at a wayside inn on the outskirts of the King's city. In the morning we are stunned to find the King of Cups walking toward us as we exit our quarters. He didn't even know we were there but he found us. It seems to be the way with the King that he is all powerful and apparently all knowing.

The King is old and frail now but he greets us as if he were still the young Prince, gracious and full of life. He shows us his kingdom and we bask in his good will. His attendant wife Polly Esther is as vociferous as always and shares recipes upon request.

Days later we fire up the blue chariot and head out, taking a different route along the Loneliest Highway in America. It reveals an equal amount of desert. We stop at Mom's Café in some town for "the best scones in the world." They weren't. They were like big, fat, floppy fried doughnuts. Since then I have been on a quest to secure the best scone recipe from the past and have succeeded in baking up some lovely morsels.

Rain pounds as Tris guides faithful Blue down the mucky back roads into Fondis. It was a valiant journey to visit a great man of immeasurable repute. I sleep for four days. Tris is now one of my favorite traveling companions. (I only have two others.)

XXXIX.

TURKEYS

Roger Rural

TURKEY: *(n)* 1. A pejorative term; 2. What should've been the National symbol; 3. A rather faraway place whose capital is the stopping point for the Orient Express; 4. A large bird that looks like a pigeon put together by a committee.

There is a "cute" book, intended for elementary school-age children, about a pathetic turkey, a bloodthirsty, witless farmer, and a bunch of first graders who keep the farmer from what looks like turning the turkey into hamburger with an axe.

When my son came home from first grade one day in November, after having read that story, he was troubled. "Daddy," he asked plaintively, "Do we raise turkeys to kill them?"

"We raise them for Thanksgiving," I replied.

"But do we kill them?"

"We don't raise them just to kill them. We raise them to eat."

The first foray I ever had with a turkey was on an April afternoon about nine months after we'd moved in. It had been a long day at work, and I was tired. Since I am prone to fits of the imagination, I honestly thought the thing strutting on my back porch was a space alien. It had a little red head and was surrounded by what I thought looked like an oversized parka.

I figured that the heat or the wind or my excessive tiredness was to blame, and even though I registered that the thing gobbled at me and walked up and down with a rasp on the floorboards of the porch, I figured that it would disappear after I took a nap.

I took a nap. It did not disappear.

There's a sort of art to raising turkeys. They start as such ridiculous sticky-outy pieces of feather and head and blinking eyes that one wonders why a merciful creator would inflict such a thing with life or expect it to fulfill its promise, only to see it ultimately wind up on a late November table. That seems almost cruel.

In raising turkey chicks, I've been told that heat is the key. "Keep 'em panting" is the advice Leroy Dean, Fair Poultry Superintendent, gives, suggesting a room temperature of ninety degrees Fahrenheit "with plenty of water for 'em."

Then, after the nights no longer cool down to nothing, about the middle of May, they go out to one of the poultry houses where they grow and grow and grow.

A stray turkey, when it is confused, struts and frets his hour upon the stage, just like Lady Macbeth, with about the same dramatic motions. It shakes its head and gobbles a lot.

So I stood to one side and studied it. I wasn't afraid it would attack me; it was too busy strutting. No; I wanted to figure out why Franklin would have ever thought that this bird, an example of American domestication on my porch, could be so noble. How could whoever domesticated the thing render it so stupid?

My reverie was cut short by the appearance of two dogs, who, tearing around the corner of the house, made for the turkey at full tilt. The turkey, startled, did not know whether to fly or run. Instead, it fell off the porch and rolled toward the dogs. I've never seen dogs more surprised. They scattered before it like a blown dandelion before recovering and trying to chase it.

Fortunately, Mrs. Rural had come home by then, and very appropriately picked up the turkey and set it in the chicken yard; breathless and minus a few feathers—the turkey, not Mrs. Rural.

"But we don't eat all the turkeys we raise, do we, Daddy?" asked my six year-old.

"No—some of them we sell," I told him. "Remember last year, when Holly paid me fifty dollars for one and I gave one to Cousin Tom? We use them as gifts, too."

"But it's not right," he reasoned, "to kill them just to give away and sell."

"Of course it is, Raul," I responded gently. "We feed them well and give them plenty of clean water, don't we? They never suffer under our care, and Michael, who processes them, makes sure they never know they'll be killed. In the story your class read, the farmer made the turkey suffer."

XL.

TALKING BOOKS

Epona Maris

It may be a blessing to have a job working with things you love, but it can be a curse, too.

After I finished college and settled into my little cabin in the woods, I had very few expenses. My income from writing poetry and stories was minimal and erratic, but it covered my basic needs. I didn't "have to" get a job, but there is a strong work ethic in this country and its tides pulled me in. I determined that, if I were to be a well-rounded person, and if I wanted personal experiences to write about, then I had to get a "real job." Every respectable writer has gone through a string of them, from dishwasher to fashion designer.

The Folios of Fondis Bookstore was looking for part-time help. I figured that would be a natural, since I love to read and being around books could inspire me to greater flights of writing. Amos Whitney owned the bookstore and was happy to hire me: "You ought to at least know how to make change without counting your toes," he said.

I learned how to work the antique cash register and how to search for books to order online. I had already searched through most of the books on the shelves. I felt proud of myself for being gainfully employed and Amos was pleased with my work so much that he took a few days off for the first time in years.

It was the first time I was in the store alone that the books started talking to me. I had been itching to pick up the latest copy of a fantasy series I enjoyed, so I took an opportunity to read a couple of pages while no customers were around. A couple of pages turned into twenty, which only ended when the bell above the door jangled. I helped an elderly woman find a birthday present for her grandson (patiently, I desperately hoped) while the fantasy book sat invitingly on the counter. "Read me," it implored. "There be dragons here..." As soon as the bell rang behind her heels, I grabbed the book and ran with it behind the stacks. The afternoon passed in alternate bursts of blissful escapism and guilty jumps at the ring of the bell.

As I passed the history section, I could here the echoes of battles and discoveries, feel the dry air of ancient tombs. When I guided a customer to the reference section, my attention was caught by the crisp voice of a dictionary, telling me the etymology of "rheumatism." I did my best to attend carefully to my customers, but, somehow, I think they noticed my lapses.

When, at last, the sun went down and I could turn the sign to say "closed," I grabbed the half-read fantasy book and settled down to read in peace. Just a little further, I told myself. Outside the store window, the bare branches of the Cottonwood trees shivered in the late October frost. It was midnight when the whispers from the horror section wormed their way into my consciousness. I think I remembered to lock the door before I ran home.

XLI.

A MAGICAL SAMHAIN

Deirdre H. Moon

Oooh, October. The airy-fairy month.
"Who says?" That's the Lady of the Lake. She always says that. Kinda airy-fairy herself. Not that I know anything about that sort of thing.
"It is the month of Halloween," states ever knowing Barbarella the Tree Queen.
"Right. Samhain," I agree, knowing those grammarians will be looking for whichs. I give it the proper Celtic pronunciation, saying *"sow' an."*
So, we'd best prepare. A celebration.
I check my lunar calendar. Halloween is also a Druid moon. Way cool. Plans evolve. We'll meet on the north of Fondis.
Hoist my skirt between my legs, tucking it into my brass belt. Hop on my mountain bike. Well, it's not my mountain bike. It's Guadalajara's mountain bike. She left it in the garage when she headed out for the Big Apple, the city named after Avalon. My cloak flies behind me.
Maneuver dirt roads at dusk hoping the miner's light on my head will warn back road drivers. By rare occurrence there are none. I pull off at the rusty filigree gate. It doesn't take too much work with my hair pin to nudge away the caked dirt and loosen resistant parts. It screeches open.
Darkness falls like a bowling ball. The headlight flickers, dies. Drat. Ditch the bike behind a rabbit brush, wonder where the Lady of the Lake and Barbarella are. Trudge reluctantly toward the trail up the ravine as a deep fog seeps out of nowhere.
Glance over both shoulders, suppress a shudder. North is to my right. The trail ahead. I think. I see nothing. Stretch my hands in front of me as my skirt snakes down my legs. I jump. Barbarella wears a watch for some unknown reason. She never looks at it. The Lady is usually prompt. Where are they? I should have asked Isis. She's always there on time.
Whose bright idea was it anyway to watch moonrise over the Bijou? A thousand coyotes howl. My breath comes

rapidly. I reach out to my sides, touch the ravine. Sand crunches under my Birkenstocks as I step forward.

One step at a time is a good philosophy. Except on a black Samhain night alone in a ravine with wild beasts lurking and who knows what kind of strange spirits.

I lift my chin, force a deep inhale. This is an adventure. Remember? I don't. Step forward. Feel. Breathe. Step. Listen. No steps follow. I wish and don't at the same moment. I dare not call their names into the blackness.

A nicker. I freeze. Do a 360. What if....? Block the thought. It's only a horse. What if he stampedes? Can one horse stampede? Get a grip, girl.

I climb to a narrow ledge, sit on a cactus. Utter unprintables.

Listen. Almost a whinny but different. Melodic, sweet. Close. Hold my breath, scan the emptiness. Dainty hoof steps in the sand. Wrap my arms around my body, wait.

A cold nose nudges my leg above woolen socks. Jump to my feet and hear him run a short distance. A second approach. Glance over my shoulder, wondering if I should climb higher. Again he backs off.

I stand perfectly still, barely breathing. A soft nose touches my palm. I slip my hand under his chin, rub. Glide my fingers up his jawline, scratch behind his ears like he was a donkey. Slip my hands across his brow and freeze.

Slowly my fingertips gaze along the horn. A unicorn. He is in my mind and I in his. He moves. I hoist myself onto his back, clutch his shimmering mane, tighten my legs to his strong body. We float up the ravine to the cliff above the Bijou.

A thousand spirits shimmer along the rim. Slipping to the earth, I press my arm across his withers, leaning into him as we watch the moonrise.

Barbarella and the Lady of the Lake arrive later with Paris Nouakchott just back from the desert.

XLII.

COMFORT

Roger Rural

Comfort: (n) *1. What a cold beer and a plate of nachos once meant after doing yard work all day; 2. Paired with "Joy," the title of a snuff film from 1936; 3. The absence of noise to anyone over age 40.*

    Every morning, coming off the Colorado Plateau into the Cherry Creek Valley, my daughter and I look for the moose, who stands about 50 yards away from the road under a clump of pines, just where a moose should be. It might be a little larger than a real moose and its black sheet metal horns and outline are certainly less bendable than a real moose would be, but its appearance and benignity give comfort to us because it looks so appealing.
    There's a comfort in looks when they're contrived: How many men my age have been comforted by the Sports Illustrated *swimsuit issue? And there's a comfort in the uncontrived.* Some twenty-five years ago, Suzanne stopped by my dorm room at the State Agricultural College as the clouds scudded across the Colorado sky, making the warm afternoon grey and purple and the sense of wonder infinite. There should have been a herd of moose on the field below and the entire city that surrounded the campus should have disappeared. Of course, it did not; but it could be ignored on such a day.
    She opened the door with the trepidation of a novice seeing Mother Superior and stood quietly until I noticed her.
    "His name is Bob and I think he likes me," she said plainly. "And he teaches my Zoology class and I think I'm in love with him."
    "Neat," I answered. I was all of nineteen then, and infected with poetry. "Come stand here and watch the day."
    She had made a decision two hours later after we had both watched night fall in silence.
    There's an Indian on a horse we can see on Fremont Road, high on a ridge above everything, looking toward Fondis. The wheat and alfalfa and weeds wave around him and he gives us comfort because he's appropriate in his setting. He would have meant danger one hundred years

ago; the same way the plunging buffalo outside Prairie Taxidermy would have stirred fear in an old-timer: today, it's curious and appropriate.

"In a hundred years, do you s'pose that what we consider fearsome will be on display?" I ask my daughter.

"Like spiders?"

"Maybe bears and mountain lions, too."

"Daddy, does that mean they won't be in the woods anymore?"

"I dunno. Maybe," I shrug, then noticing some movement just outside my headlights, I slow down suddenly and stop the car, taking it out of gear. "Look, Rachel! Deer!" And they are the real thing, thirty feet ahead of us, in the cold November morning darkness, crossing the road, bounding from one fence to another.

"Yeah," she marvels at their grace. Their appearance is rare enough to give us both pause.

"Neat," I say, putting the car in gear again. *Funny, that was the same thing I said when my friend Suzanne told me she was going to marry Bob.*

XLIII.

HUNTING WORDS

Epona Maris

I met him first during the coldest day of the dying year, so that is when I tend to look for him again. I have seen him walking the autumn hills more often though, and that is when I first talked to him. Him: the Hunter, I call him, because I don't know his true name. Deirdre has a nodding acquaintance with him and says the faeries refer to "Himself" at times, but she knows no other name.

The first time, I followed snow tracks of elk to a clearing and found him standing, as if listening to the wind. I wasn't sure if I should speak. He held a recurve bow with an arrow nocked, the string slightly drawn. While I hesitated, cold and wondering what to do, he looked at me and smiled. I smiled back, without thinking, but he was gone before I could speak.

Since that day, I have thought about him when the cold wind blows dry leaves through the Fondis hills. Who is he, what is he hunting, and why did he smile at me, then leave? I asked Deirdre about it, but she just shrugged, dismissing it as male behavior. The Lady of the Lake was equally as vague: I should think of why I happened upon that clearing in the woods at just that time in my life. Barbarella worked my numbers for the date, but it made no sense to me. I was sure that it should make sense, somehow. Make sense to me, if no one else.

I have thought often about the different way men and women conceive of the flow of conversation. Men tend to see it as a linear thing: query and response, statement and contradiction, followed by challenge and counter-challenge. Men are direct, yet still say less than they mean. Women are different.

Deirdre is the most nearly direct of my usual female conversationalists, but even she relies on discursion to emphasize a point. At first, I thought that Barbarella was hopelessly tangential, until I realized that she was weaving words: there are definite warp threads in her speech, but the weft threads, which make the pattern, are sometimes threaded in, sometimes left to dangle until the picture she weaves requires them to be complete. The Lady of the Lake leaves resonant spaces for other's speech to fill with meaning. I won't even begin to describe the way Showelreth Foxfire spins language into braided lace. I have always been more to the point, despite my reputation for spontaneous poetry. And so I am challenged by one who speaks to me without speaking.

The first time he did speak words to me was on a late October evening, as I was returning home from the hills. I came across him sitting by a campfire in a sheltered hollow, his bow unstrung by his feet. I stopped short, but he beckoned for me to sit by the fire, so I did. We observed each other for a moment, as the clouds slid across the face of the moon.

"Who are you?" I asked, then doubted my directness. He just smiled and added wood to the fire.

"Who do you think I am?" he asked.

"Someone from my wildest dreams," I answered, thinking of the Moody Blues song. He laughed and I thought I could trace faint moonlight along antlers above his head.

"Dreams are real," he answered. I know that, but didn't say it. The evening passed with no more words.

XLIV.

WORMHOLES & SLOT MACHINES

Deirdre H. Moon

Sometimes you have to leave Fondis to appreciate it.

I wasn't planning on traveling. I was content with quiet mornings, snuggling with Merlin cat, lazy noontimes munching an apple and talking to the faeries, a leisurely siesta followed by a bike ride to Cerridwen's for tea time and long conversations delving into Celtic philosophy when Epona Maris might join us.

Circumstances required that I travel. When I was mindless and clueless, She Who Knows All (of course she doesn't) said we must go. Numb, I nodded. Of course. I mean, sometimes she is right.

We set off in a sparkling blue Rent A Chariot and headed west, stopping that first day to renew our bodies with the Water Spirits in Glenwood Springs. Driving on I was certain that most of the western United States was desert. The barren moonscape shimmered in the sun's scorching heat. There must be desert faeries but I couldn't find them.

The next day we hit a vortex. She Who Knows All was at the wheel, dizzy, not tracking. "Pull off," I commanded. Jumping from the vehicle, I grabbed a water bottle, forced her head between her legs, poured water along her neck. Then we walked into the sage and I plucked a sprig and she inhaled the pungent aroma.

"We're in a wormhole," she mumbled. Time compressed, depressed. Space contracted. I didn't have a clue where we were. Later she wrote "vortex" on the map so we'd know to be aware when we passed that way again.

Much later we are trapped in a maze of Slot Machine Hell. Frantic neon lights hammered the atmosphere into staccatic blindness. Ear damaging racket blasted like lasers across the madness of a casino.

Eventually we can attend the dying King of Swords.

Finally we escape in our chariot, seeking green, and water. Big water.

I walk out on a pier beneath the Golden Gate Bridge, soothed by the lapping of waves, renewed by the salt air, blessed by the beauty of coastal faeries dancing a welcome.

Eucalyptus trees heal my heart with their steady magnificence. I walk in the dim forest of redwoods, shielded by the canopy.

Much later I return to my yurt on the ridge above Fondis to contemplate the journey, glad at last to be home. There is magic everywhere but it seems easier to access under the rainbow over the Bijou where the otherworld merges gracefully with what we call reality.

What is real? Is the unreal not as true as the real? The faeries giggle and dance a reel.

Winter

WINTER LIGHT

Epona Maris

In the Winter I tend to walk less frequently
And follow familiar trails,
Patterning the same steps into the fallen snow.
Indoors, the sun slants lower and longer,
Touching to life objects on the far wall
That remain unnoticed in more straight-forward months.
Hard to believe that the hard ground holds
Forgotten bulbs of flowers
Stashed away in Fall
Into savings accounts that reward only
If you leave them quiet until Spring.

When my days are cold
And walk the same pattern into my life,
I watch my thoughts slant lower and longer
Into unnoticed windows, touching
Into life memories I had forgotten
During busier times.
Hard to believe that this hard ground holds
Forgotten depths of feeling
That can take root and blossom
In their own time.

As I pattern my days here,
I have watched, for some friends,
The fire burn low, needing other fuel,
Other hands to stir the ashes back to life.
I have watched some friends blaze
With hearts hot enough to burn diamonds into coal—
But I have mourned enough ashes in my time.
All the while, when some friends flame out and down,
And others leave for warmer dreams,
Speaking sadly of the limits, the cold and barrenness
Of winter here,
I see a few who simply remain
And transcend.

XLV.

THE NIGHT THE ANIMALS TALK

Deirdre H. Moon

Comes the month of magic. The month we think we are diving into the abyss because we are abandoned by the sun, bereft of warmth.

Fear not, giggle the faeries of Fondis. They chatter all the time if you listen. I don't. I forget. But that old crone out there in lala-land listens and she tells it good.

The Unknown Hierophant and the Lady of the Lake picked me up in a gigantic truck. I groped at a ladder to climb in. We drove through a blizzard, picked up Barbarella and Paris Nouakchott, who of course fed us a scrumptious gourmet meal.

Then we headed out to see the white haired wild woman who lives in a log cabin on the edge of Fondis. She reminded us that there is truth in everything and we must open our hearts to listen. I think I was complaining about the weather and the short days and all that stuff that nags us during the holidays.

She walks the woods in her ratty green cloak, her hair flying crazy in the wind, her old boots crunching snow. She says she listens. I've seen her stop and put out her hand so birds may land. I really went out there for a tarot reading but she said the stars weren't right. I had to do it on my own. Drat.

Who is she? You probably wouldn't recognize her. She rarely goes to the local market. She's pretty much of a hermit. First time I met her years ago, she was meditating for world peace around a feeble fire in the middle of a teepee while the snow blew and the thermometer shivered below zero. Calls herself Snow Raven. We all call her Cerridwen.

Last month she worked with the energies for Harmonic Concordance, inviting the Lady of the Lake, Barbarella the Tree Queen, Mystic Mercedes, Paris Nouakchott and I for tea and scones, the latest Fondis fad.

Now we are here in Fondis on Christmas eve and Cerridwen gives us the scoop on December, being not just Solstice, Christmas, Chanukah, Boxing Day or Kwanza, but a time to really tune into the animal kingdom. I perked up, missing my old cat Amberber Nefertiti Amberlini who now romps in Kitty Heaven. I'll have a chat with Merlin when I get back to the yurt.

Beatrice Potter told us all about it if you remember your delicate literature from childhood. The animals talk. Really.

I was a little skeptical at first. We traipsed through the shivering woods following the old wise woman. She led us to the animals.

I listened. Now, here's the cool thing. I looked into the limpid brown eyes of that regal beast Basalt, a well regarded, as well as self important, llama. I knew he'd talk to me. Aloof, he will not allow me into his mind.

On that night when the animals talk, he spoke. We all heard him. The former King of Sirius agreed to come to this planet to connect with the souls that he meets. Some call him arrogant. He simply doesn't have time to engage in the mundane. After all, he really is a king, not some plebian who knows naught.

On the night the animals talk, Basalt, King of Sirius spoke for them all. There had been a council meeting of all the animals in the Fondis region. They are very concerned about the impact of a proposed new superslab just west of Fondis.

He frowned. Really. He's seen it all before. "Beware. We work in harmony with the earth. It is up to the humans to protect the land and the animals from invasion of noise pollution, air pollution and environmental damage." He said those words. Me, being one of the humans, felt guilty.

We left in a somber mood, quietly acknowledging the return of light and the responsibility offered us by a great one. Cerridwen chuckled and nodded her wild hair.

XLVI.

CHRISTMAS EVE FOR THE FAMILY

Roger Rural

Family: *(n)* 1. People who share a common characteristic, such as a bulbous nose and sometimes the same last name; 2. The folks you meet at funerals; 3. People who keep borrowing stuff from you, like your barbecue grill and frilly underwear and never give them back.

It was Shelby's job to buy the turkey and cook it; Biff would handle everything else: vegetables, soup, and dessert. They were both up at six the morning before Christmas Eve: Shelby doing the laundry and Biff cleaning the hallway and bedrooms; Shelby would clean the bathroom and kitchen later.

About ten o'clock, Biff set out to buy the vegetables, leaving Shelby fussing with the tree and answering the occasional phone calls from well-wishers and friends: "You know that Steven died," Peter intoned. "Yeah, last night. His mom's not taking it real well."

"Anything we can do?" Shelby asked.

Peter didn't think so. "Funeral's on Saturday, we think. I'll call you."

Shelby paused briefly to cross Steven's name and number from the list he kept by the phone, a list entitled "Retrovere Test Group #1." Fifteen of the original fifty were gone just this year: all of them given various doses of this new drug meant to combat their shared disease.

Shelby stepped out and made sure the walkway was clear to the front porch, then assuaged the anger he felt rising in him by hurriedly dusting the furniture in the living room and dining room, lingering briefly over the reflection he saw on the dining table: he looked rather cadaverous, with sunken eyes still bright. And it was Christmas, he told himself. At eleven, he put the turkey into the roasting pan and opened the oven.

Biff huffed back with the groceries, painstakingly carrying one bag at a time up the steps and into the kitchen for a total of three trips, then busied himself at the table reading a cookbook while he regained his breath. Soon, he was whirring and stirring at the counter, chopping and grating. He went to the neighbor's to get an extra egg while Shelby, seated in a living room armchair, took a half-hour catnap.

By four, the table was set and Shelby asked Biff to "knock off" for a little while. Shelby would stir the soup and check on the vegetables. He set out the plates for twelve and melted the candle bottoms firmly into the candleholders so they wouldn't slant. He called to Biff that the half hour was over. It was precisely three o'clock. They both swallowed their Retrovere pills. Biff groggily went to shower.

While Biff crisply knotted his tie and made sure the collar was just so, Shelby basted the turkey for the tenth time and checked the consistency of the stuffing. Biff came downstairs again. Shelby headed up to shower and put on the clothes Biff had laid out for him. He was grateful that Biff had taste and understood color, but the buttons on the shirt were hard to manipulate with his angular fingers because they felt numb.

The crab-stuffed mushrooms were almost ready when Shelby descended to the kitchen and in short order, the family arrived: all ten who were not otherwise disposed or invited elsewhere: a dull array of white collar workers: good in their various jobs and very professional, but little ease at small talk. They milled around, explored the house, asked if they could help, and generally got underfoot in their newly-discovered roles as guests.

At exactly five-thirty, Shelby and Biff started serving. Their food was good and plentiful. Mercifully, conversation lagged and died altogether except for a recitation of recipes and cooking techniques. Shelby mentioned briefly that Steven had died the night before, then he asked that everyone help clear the table.

Washing and drying and putting food away was something that Shelby's and Biff's family was good at doing and by seven-thirty, the chores were done.

A few hugs were exchanged; a couple of presents passed hands. Shelby and Biff shook hands with brothers and cousins, then wished everyone a Merry Christmas. By eight o'clock, they'd both retired for the night. Their family members scattered to their various homes or parties or church services.

Holding a Christmas Eve dinner for family was important to Biff and Shelby, even though their family was more to be endured than enjoyed.

That sentiment still confounds me, some twelve years later, since they both died, numbers forty and forty two on the "Retrovere Test #1" list, some nine months later, of the same shared disease.

XLVII.

CRANKING BY HAND

Epona Maris

Sarah lay naked and sweating on the bed with the window thrown open to the frigid winter air. She did her best to ignore the whines of her three children, unsupervised on the other side of the bedroom door. "It isn't fair," she thought, over and over again. Menopausal symptoms at age 39, with two children still in diapers, was beyond what any mortal should be asked to bear. It certainly was not the life she had envisioned when she finally found Mr. Right and settled down with him to raise a family five years ago.

"Mommy, when are you coming out?" she heard her eldest ask, his mouth pressed to the door crack. Behind him, she heard a muffled shriek, a crash, then wailing cries. Sarah leaped out of bed, feeling the fires within her flesh rage as she ran to throw the door open. If the bathrobe had not been hanging on the door knob, she most likely would not have thought to put it on first.

Mr. Right, more commonly known as Nick to most of us in Fondis, came home from work to the spectacle of his wife loosely draped in a bathrobe, wild hair flying as she towered over three cowering toddlers and screamed incoherently at them. The scene was accented by glittering shards of glass on the floor and scattered papers that gently ruffled in the cold breeze.

"Uh, why is the window open?" was the first thing he could think to say.

"Who are you to complain—you're never here!" Sarah screamed at him. "I'm leaving!" She thrust her bare feet into waiting boots, grabbed the car keys from the hook, then slammed the door behind her.

Sarah was five miles down the icy road before her brain cooled enough to wonder what she would do next. She had no money, no ID, no clothes beyond a bathrobe and boots. Now that the hotflash was wearing off, she was acutely aware that it was a winter evening.

She saw the lights of my cabin appear among the trees, and that's were I come into this little story. I was busy preparing goat milk to run through the cream separator when Sarah arrived at my door, disheveled and drooping. She spilled out her story as I heated milk on the woodstove and set up the hand-cranked separator. "I don't know what to do!" she wailed. "I can't go anywhere without clothes."

"So go home," I suggested.

"I can't do that—it would be just as bad as when I left." I tested the milk temperature and made sure everything I needed was ready to go. As I listened to Sarah complain about her life, I got an inspiration.

"You know," I said, "they say that exercise is the best thing for managing hotflashes." She looked at me in surprise as I showed her how to turn the crank at a steady clip while I poured the pans of hot milk into the basin and let it flow through the separating cones into the empty bowls, one for skim milk, one for cream.

Sarah grew quiet, cranking steadily as I switched out the full bowls of milk and replaced them with empty ones. It takes awhile to separate a large batch of milk and her arm muscles were doing the complaining by the time Nick arrived at my door, surrounded by little children.

"I'm sorry," he told Sarah. "I'll try to do better." She just cried and said she was sorry, too. The kids cried just for bonding purposes, I guess.

"Wait a minute," I said. "I just need someone to crank a little bit longer." They paid no attention to me, so I had to finish the job as I usually do, cranking with one hand and pouring with the other. At least I didn't have to do the whole job by myself this time.

XLVIII.

SASSY

Deirdre H. Moon

If you know Sassy Cambridge, and everyone in Fondis knows Sassy Cambridge, then you know why I was a little uneasy about her arrival.

Sassy is a reporter for the *Fondis Daily News* and is always sticking her tape recorder in somebody's face and taking unsightly photos of them and quoting them way too accurately so they can't deny saying what they really said.

It's not that I don't like Sassy. I do. It's just that she's so, what can I say? Skeptical? Definitely skeptical. Unimaginative? Yes, unimaginative. She harbors no skill for discerning the unseen. She thinks I'm full of hocus pocus or some such unflattering judgment. So, I am anxious about her arrival.

I was surprised when she called and said she wanted to do a story on the yurt. I'd read some of her series on unusual houses in Fondis. I didn't think I really qualified. I know lots of folks who live in yurts. Of course they're not in Fondis. They're probably more yurts in the blue states. I hate how the country has been divided by red and blue. Because really, I think I live in a rainbow and I'd like the state to live there too. It won't. I'd have to move. To one of the blue states, which are really rainbow states.

But I digress. I took some Rescue Remedy and went through my Tai Chi form and still felt unbalanced. Well, that's what being in a Hanged Woman year will do to you. So, I decided to treat it homeopathically. I walked out to my favorite pine tree, climbed to the second branch and settled, looking out over the Bijou, watching Fondis in the distance. It was all as it should be.

Then I slipped across the branch below, sliding down 'til my knees clutched the bark and let go of my hands, hanging upside down. Everything looked different. My hair flowed toward the earth, picking up vibrations that my feet forget to register. Indeed, a Hanged Woman year means looking at things in a different way. And surrender. I surrendered to the bark biting against my leggings into flesh.

And I surrendered to the sound of a vehicle. Sassy, lugging a heavy camera bag, walked down the path followed by Victoria. I'd invited Victoria to join us, thinking it might ease my way with Sassy.

We broke the ice with donkey talk; Burrito winning them over, I think. Inside the yurt, I served tea and answered her persistent questions while Sassy kept taking pictures. I was distracted the entire time by the holes in her aura. I did a tarot reading for both of them. Some strange things were going on in their lives. It was all there in the cards. She thought it was all in the photographs. I didn't know if we'd ever be friends, Sassy and I. Victoria held us together without even knowing it.

I was frazzled when they left and went into a head stand for ten minutes to calm myself. Staying centered in life is a challenge even when you live high above Fondis with a view toward Kansas and a donkey who brays a greeting to each passing dawn.

XLIX.

APPROPRIATE WRAPPING:
Observations of Christmas and Beyond

Roger Rural

WRAPPING: *(n, v)1. The name applied to a primitive genre of poetry; 2. The outward apparel of a gift or token; 3. The first name of the famous Puritan Evangelist, Wrapping Paper, whose sermons against wickedness were read quite seriously until readers looked at his name.*

A twenty foot roll of Christmas wrapping paper looks like a tsunami on the dining room table, threatening everything in its path and inconveniently hiding the tools to tame it: scissors and tape.

"I'm lousy at measuring," I tell Rachel, who wants the box for Mommy, six inches by eighteen inches by six inches, to look appropriate; housing, as it does, the two brass turtle ashtrays she chose at the consignment store. The box is a little big for them: thirty times too large, in fact. The turtles clank and slide as I roll the package over the wrapping paper, trying to measure as I saw professional wrappers do it in an exclusive gift shop where I worked some twenty years ago. Rachel, of course, does not know she's chosen two ashtrays for her mommy. All she sees is the brasswork. Her intention, in choosing a large box, is to create pleasant surprise: a fine Christmas intention.

"Were you drunk when you wrapped this?" Louise asked me in a way that was not unkindly for her, since she'd gone from a childhood of shoveling cow manure on a dairy farm to marrying men for profitable gain. Appropriate wrapping, for her, meant a decent figure after fifty and a personality that adapted to the man she married. My Uncle Fletch encouraged her to be direct and run affairs as she chose. It was Christmas Eve and she'd invited his family members to enjoy her hospitality. Mindful of her blue and white decorating scheme, I'd combed antique shops in Fondis to find something that would fit in, finally deciding on a Delft plate. I carefully packed it in newspaper, then botched the job of wrapping by folding all my corners at odd angles and leaving one side of the box, which proclaimed: MOTOR OIL: 10-w30, exposed.

"Thank-you," she said graciously as she removed the plate, glancing at it as she placed it on a tall shelf in the kitchen, then she refilled her drink of scotch and water. "Now your turn," she said, handing me a thin long box, appropriately wrapped. It was a tie. It had a store label and a brown pattern. I have five of those ties that Louise gave me: all in the same brown pattern, all appropriately wrapped, each marking a different Christmas Eve: 1981, 1982, 1983, 1986, and 1990.

Because appropriate wrapping is required at Poultry exhibitions, I make certain my son is dressed in a white shirt and dark slacks when he shows his geese and turkeys. Because appropriate wrapping at Christmas means a great deal to my daughter, I grit my teeth and watch her chop the paper irregularly. Because appropriate wrapping is something that's important to her, she has dresses to wear to birthday parties. Because appropriate wrapping is important to me in the workplace, I tend to think little of colleagues who are trying to look younger than they are. One, who has continually enriched her plastic surgeon, is desperately trying to regain the skin and body she had when fifteen, some forty years before.

"Daddy," Rachel said doubtfully, turning the paper square we'd cut, "I think this might be too small."

A well-wrapped package, a sign above the professional wrappers proclaimed, *should bring joy to its receiver*, and I remember thinking about a corporate client, burdened by another Waterford or Orrefors paperweight, being so enraptured with the wrapping that he wouldn't bother to unwrap it; just admire its outside, and it would sit, like my brown ties from all those Christmas Eves, gathering dust. Obviously, Mommy's package, as my daughter and I wrapped it, with its miles of tape, its odd folding, and its attempt at sprightliness with a plastic red bow, would only bring despair to the receiver. But my partner's resilient. Besides, the part that wasn't wrapped was underneath the box, and proclaimed loudly: CHEESE: KEEP REFRIGERATED.

Probably the most appropriate wrapping and gift together came about the Christmas my son, Raul, was three. We were at Louise's again, and I presented her with an appropriately wrapped package of food, in which were a couple of pounds of bacon and sausage I had raised that year. THRIFTY DOLLAR, *the bag proclaimed. She stiffened, graciously accepted the gift, popped it in the freezer, then ran off to the nether regions of her house. She returned moments later, bearing an appropriately wrapped box, with just as appropriately written* SEASON'S GREETINGS *card on it, which she presented to Raul. She then freshened her scotch and water. Sometimes, appropriate wrapping doesn't hide the gift inside.*

On Christmas Day, Raul opened the package, which contained a "snakelight:" a flashlight with a long bendable arm, capable of being twisted in tight places. Raul loved it. On the back of the card, we found the following: "To Louise with love, from Amy." Louise had merely taped the card more firmly to the package.

Rachel had very carefully wrapped my package this Christmas with a gift that doesn't match my decorating or taste, but it's special because she chose it: a green, porcelain duck. It sits on top of this computer where I look at it everyday.

L.

EARTH SECRETS

Deirdre H. Moon

Shhh. There are secrets in Fondis.

Some of them have been blasted in statewide headlines like the self important principal who got busted in a budget scandal.

But there are other secrets that bring light and smiles when discovered.

There's a magical room in Fondis, tucked away behind red doors that Harry Potter might wish to explore.

Doors into mystery and self discovery.

I slip through the side door of the old stone building, climb the stairs using the child height railing. Pause at the half open red door, curious.

Afternoon light climbs through the bank of windows on the north wall. "You are what you think." Chalk written on the greenboard. Wild African drums pound from the CD. An array of long, paper covered tables. Teenagers intent on creation. My inner child giggles. I hesitate.

I ease into the room, scope it out.

Clay calls. Hunks of dark green globs, the energy within singing my name. Clay, the invitation of the Earth Mother reaching for me.

"There is no right or wrong." That's the voice of the Clay Master speaking. (Shouldn't it be mistress? Goddess?) The teacher.

I find a place next to a young man making an African clay drum.

I stare at the unformed clay. Wonder. Listen. Let go of the room, the others, the dragging strings of the mundane.

The clay is subtle. My mind steps back. My fingers and the clay communicate. Nothing else exists.

She lies within, waiting. The Snake Goddess. Waiting for form. Waiting since before Helen of Troy saw a horse.

Snake Goddess nurturing the young squirming spirals of life between her breasts. Snake as transformation. Clay ready to transform and welcome the return of the goddess.

My hands pull her forth. I watch. She emerges. And then she waits. Again.

Time passes. I forget her. She does not forget me. I forget the room of creativity, the secret of Fondis.

Medusa's daughter reminds me. The clay sculpture is unfinished. Honor the Snake Goddess with completion.

I return to the red doors, the room of mystery and art. Catch a ride with the Lady of the Lake. Barbarella, the Tree Queen, doesn't want to go with us. I am to learn alchemy.

How can you know what will happen in the realm of the salamanders where the Fire Faeries dance with color in a kiln and what was unknown becomes known?

The Snake Goddess rises as if from water instead of fire. She is neither and both. Alchemy comes from the chemistry of glazes. Color on color. Thick. Color and heat and the eventual alchemy when she speaks, acknowledging form.

Who else calls from the clay? My hands listen. I wait.

Now the Snake Goddess hovers at the stargate over Fondis, protecting all future transformations.

The secret is out. The Goddess is in.

LI.

SHOVELING

Roger Rural

SHOVEL: *(n, vb)* 1. The thing you use to trench, dig, and kill snakes; 2. The thing you do to clean your child's room; 3. Admiral Sir Cloudsely Shovel was a rough man whose ship ran aground outside Plymouth, England. I think it killed him.

I have a pair of boots I wear just for this task because they're warm and water repellent and have deep treads. I wear them just for snow because they're made for it; not for indoor use at all.

Sally called. She told me her former husband had taken their eldest son to Florida and they were going to be gone most of the week when the son was supposed to be in school. Sally painted a grim picture of late night parties, a rented sports car, deep-sea fishing, lots of beer and mixed drinks, and single, very eligible women: a grim scenario, if there ever was one, for a fifteen year old male. If this was a form of abuse, I suggested she call Florida Social Services. If this was a kidnapping, I suggested she call the police. She never did either.

There was a whole lot of stuff that came down in the night, leaving a huge pile at the foot of the driveway and a hill only a few feet from the garage. It was difficult to walk through and I'd only get the car stuck if I tried to negotiate it head on. So I got out the shovel, one of those light plastic jobs that looks like a coal scoop, hoping to reduce the hill somewhat. I prefer to use a lighter shovel; the snow flies farther with less effort.

Sally again: Those pesky Social Services people had told her that it was unwise for her to sleep in the same bed with her two younger boys, but that they should have their own beds. Did I have some beds I wasn't using?

As a matter of fact, I knew just where I could get a couple of beds whose owner would give them to me if I'd just haul them away. So, I loaded the truck with them: headboards, rails, mattresses, and boxsprings, and called Sally. Where should I deliver them? I could do it the next day, although I knew that the drive to her house would be a couple of hours.

"Isn't that funny?" she asked. "I just found a couple of beds stored in our basement! No; we won't be needing your beds after all. Isn't it wonderful?"

I should've just called some charitable outfit to take them away. Instead, I dithered by putting the extra beds in my own basement, where they did a marvelous job of soaking up the water when we had a flood. My son and I then tore them up and put them in trashcans. It's amazing how many trashcans a mattress can fill.

There are very few times I bother anymore about clearing a path to our door. If someone's expected, I shovel it; otherwise, I just leave it. Too much trouble. Same way with the path from the backdoor to the barn. I clear what's necessary: the threshold, for instance, so ice and snow don't cake under the door, making it impossible to shut properly. The rest I leave, first to get trampled by the dog, then by my son, Raul, carrying coffee cans full of water for the chickens and ducks, and lastly, by me, carrying half a bale of hay from the garage to the barn, where the goats, sheep, and llama tear it apart. The animals don't bother with the depth of the snow; they deal with it.

"I really appreciate your asking if Simon can attend Raul's birthday sleepover," Sally told me, "But what with the divorce and all, he's gotten kind of clingy, and what if he wakes up at two in the morning and wants me?"

"Well—last year, when we had a similar party, none of the boys over here seemed to notice that they had parents, Sally."

"Well—"she said, hesitating. "I think it would be good another time. Besides—this weekend, we've been invited to my lover's parent's house in Estes Park. It might be real hard for Simon—"

"I imagine it would be, Sally. Perhaps next year, Raul will invite Simon to his ninth birthday party."

When we first moved here to Fondis, I bought a snowblower that stood in splendor in the garage when it wasn't being used. It always got in the way and required looking after; even when it wasn't in use. The sparkplug needed changing; the exhaust got cracked on some rocks. It was just more trouble than it was worth. I figured I'd take my chances with a fold-out shovel in the trunk and a running start down the driveway, which is a lot simpler.

When Sally called, last time, around 5:30 on a grainy December evening, I watched the snowflakes swirl around *the icy ruts in the driveway, and all I could think of was shoveling, even though I tried mightily to listen to her story about how her eldest son had been arrested on charges of petty theft.*

I had snow to shovel. I wasn't interested in anything else.

LII.

WINTERGREEN

Epona Maris

January is a month of stark contrasts: bare black branches and snow-blanketed ground; long, still nights and brief glimpses of sunshine; colorful seed catalogues and frozen ground. We are all dreamers in January, perhaps because the nights are so long. It is a time for contemplation of past and future, resolutions broken and gardens yet to come. The brave lights of December have been put away and the shadows refill the spaces between homes, separating us from each other.

I was reading seed catalogues by the wood stove in my cabin, with a cup of tea on the table and my feet warm and cozy in homemade socks, when the radio went off. "Fondis Fire, respond to 1124 Cherrybark Drive on report of an 85 year-old female unconscious with hypothermia."

I pulled on boots and coat and was out the door without thinking, my EMT bag in hand. I revved the engine in my truck to kick it out of frozen hibernation, then was halfway down my driveway before the dispatch information kicked into my frozen brain. That was the address of the woman most of the Bijou basin called Granny June. I had no idea how old she was, but 85 was a safe bet. I drove as fast as I dared down the icy dirt roads, thinking of her frequent laugh, the wealth of cookies that spilled from her kitchen and the slips of geraniums that she gave to anyone who asked.

When the ambulance pulled up to the little bungalow on Cherrybark Drive, we could see the front door open to the cold. We were met just inside by Laura, Granny June's sixty-something daughter.

"She didn't answer when I called, so I came over to check on her," Laura told us. "Her pain's been getting worse, lately—she's hardly been getting out of bed. She said the cold eats at her bones. Well, when I got here, the front door was open and it was freezing cold in here. I've been trying to warm her up, but she won't move." She led us to a quilt-bundled figure in the rocking chair. Granny June was sitting there, eyes closed, feet propped up in front of the cold wood stove, looking peaceful.

I touched her face, then felt for a carotid pulse as Dan set up the heart monitor. I could tell she was dead, but the rule is that no one is really dead until they're warm and dead. We packed her armpits and groin with heat packs and rewrapped her in the quilt. The thought finally hit me: "Why is the heat off?" I asked Laura. She checked the thermostat.

"It was turned off," she said. I heard the roar of the furnace as she turned the dial up. When Laura turned to look at us, she was crying. "I don't understand," she said. "The heat was turned off, the front door was propped open, there's no fire in the stove, but she just sat there."

We all looked at the tiny woman in the rocking chair, who must have waited patiently for death to come. Granny June must have been reading her seed catalogues because they were piled up on the reading table next to her chair. I glanced at the top one, then picked it up to look closer. Next to a picture of Wintergreen, she had written: "There is a time for everything. Don't make a big fuss over me, because I had a good time while I was here."

It was well after midnight before I made it back home, but I wasn't ready to go to sleep. I built the fire up in the wood stove, put the kettle on it and went through the seed catalogues. I turned to the herb pages and looked for Wintergreen, then got my pen and started writing:

"*Good bye Granny June,*
Green heart that grows strong
Despite winter's snow,
Sheltered in the hearts of those you love..."

LIII.

FONDIS FAERIES

Deirdre H. Moon

"You wanna see fairies, I'll show you fairies," my friend Joe teased, pulling off at Colorado Spring's oldest gay bar. He tossed a couple of brews. I shot a kamikaze, checked it out. I like gay bars. Nobody hits on me. This was certainly different than Bijou After Dark, where I used to hang in Fondis.

You know Fondis fell off the map in '53, back in the last century. Now you can get a tornado warning on line from the National Weather Service about what's threatening Fondis. Things change.

But not everything. The faeries are still in Fondis. I wanted to tell Joe about faeries but he wasn't in the mood.

Some people think faeries are fantasy but they're just not looking. Faeries are everywhere if you sit back, soften your focus and peer into the other realm. It's not just Ireland and Scotland who host the sparkling, wispy creatures. And you don't need any mind-altering substances to bring them into focus.

I first noticed them when I was four years old. I was sitting quietly on a ledge in the misty realm of my childhood. Blue flowers swayed in the breeze, shimmered. That's when I saw the energy beings flitting about my secret hiding place.

Faeries, not to be confused with fairies. Although fairies are really in now that Queer Eye for the Straight Guy is all the rage. Joe thinks it's about time. He finally acknowledged faeries of the fey one day when he came to visit.

At dusk, we walked along the edge of Fondis Lake. Shadows and shimmering gold light played in the water. In a rainbow twinkle, a sweet water faerie danced among the reeds, lilting about, in and out. Joe saw her too and grinned quietly to me.

Often when I go to visit the old crone Cerridwen, we walk in the woods on the edge of Fondis and watch the faeries dance. Sometimes Lightheart comes along. She brings a parcel of faeries with her wherever she goes. We all do, I suppose. We just forget to look for them.

One day the Lady of the Lake and I were pondering a tarot spread and there they were. The faeries. Right there on the border of the cards, twirling and giggling and shouting out truths. Or distractions. I wasn't sure.

Fairies and faeries are both with us and it will ease the way of the world if we can accept them all with love. Easier said than done some days. A goal to ponder.

LIV.

KAREN'S LIST

Roger Rural

LIST: *(n,v)* 1. What an ocean liner does with too much stuff on the starboard side; 2. What a passenger does on an ocean liner with too much stuff in him; 3. Items, usu. in some sequential order, e.g.: Dog Food, Scallions, Anti-itch powder, etc.; 4. What Santa Claus has among the "naughty" and "nice" categories.

> *"I was thirty. Before me stretched the portentous, menacing road of a new decade...Thirty—the promise of a decade of loneliness, a thinning list of single men to know, a thinning briefcase of enthusiasm, thinning hair..."* (The Great Gatsby, by F. Scott Fitzgerald)

Could her future partner have children? Karen wondered. Yes; but with the provision that they were adolescents or older. NO CHILDREN UNDER THIRTEEN, she wrote.

She was making the list of her needs on the advice of Deirdre, her sort of spiritual adviser, who'd said, over coffee that morning, "I know that you've wanted a man in your life for a few years. Now is the time to make the list. Put down what you want and don't want. Be completely honest. You're ready for it. And if you're honest—"Deirdre raised her eyebrows suggestively "—The spirits will know and work for you."

Deirdre had said no more about it; just gathered her silks about her, flung her luxurious red hair behind her, paid for coffee, and headed for the Fondis Womyn's Centre, where she worked as Executive Director.

Ten years ago, Karen reflected, she would've thought of Deirdre H. Moon as seriously unbalanced; but owing to her own honesty about her vulnerabilities, she'd come to accept Deirdre, who saw through everybody.

What age should he be? Karen had just turned forty-three and she wasn't sure a guy under forty would fill the bill. In their thirties, most men would be establishing themselves in their careers; in their twenties, most men would be casting about for careers. SOMEWHERE

BETWEEN FORTY AND FIFTY, she wrote. Someone, she reflected, who remembered when Kennedy was assassinated.

Divorced? Yeah, that was okay. Once: youthful indiscretion. Twice? No. It indicated an unwillingness to grow up. SINGLE OR ONCE DIVORCED, she wrote.

Pam, Karen's assistant, tapped on the doorframe, a couple of mortgage applications in hand, which she gracefully placed on Karen's desk, twirled, and walked out again. Pam had been a Jupp, Karen remembered, of a numerous clan on the eastern edge of the county, who were noted mainly for not being notable: dull brown eyes; nondescript; with dirty blonde hair. The family managed to avoid public scrutiny in general by avoiding notice outside of an occasional barfight or a record sale at the 4-H auction of a pig or a steer. When they married, it was usually to other nondescript people who attended their church.

But Pam was different. She had the same vague hair color and the same brown eyes of her tribe, but her eyes were bright and she carried herself as if she were constantly in motion. She made a good assistant, Karen knew, because she could handle closings assertively and negotiate interest rates with any lender.

"Tough as nails," one customer remarked. "Stubborn." If Pam had been a man, Karen thought, she would have been admired for these qualities, as well as her ability at detail work. Karen was lucky to have her. She hoped Pam's husband, Mark, appreciated those abilities. Pam was helping him get through Law School. His Bar exam was in June.

What sort of a job should Karen's potential mate have? She was sick of the real-estate bachelors she knew, because even if they were refined or had other interests, eventually their conversations would turn back to property and deals and how much money they made. NO SALES, she wrote. Should her future mate have a college degree? God knows, some of the most interesting men she'd ever met did not have college degrees but had mastered their trades so well that they were virtual artists at what they did, and could enjoy what Deirdre called "the spiritual side."

A piece of copper tubing in the hands of Ross, the plumber, she recalled, became a living thing as he shaped it, cut it, sanded and soldered it to fit a broken joint, all the while singing some obscure Renaissance tune by William Drummond of Hawthornden. Oh yes: he entertained regularly every summer at the Renaissance Festival in Larkspur; and oh yes, when he got mad at Dale, who never paid his bills on time, Ross managed to reroute the plumbing so the toilet flushed hot water. She liked that. SKILLED, THOUGHTFUL, MISCHIEVOUS, she wrote. COLLEGE DEGREE NOT REQUIRED. She could talk about literature with Ross, who, she later discovered, had just about finished a college degree before being dragged into his father's business after an economic downturn.

She thought of her own Fine Arts degree. Not quite the mortgage business, really; but her sense of design and color had enlivened the office, and the paintings she displayed on the walls were stunning. MUST USE HIS SPARE TIME CREATIVELY, she wrote. NO COUCH POTATO. But that would mean that she might find a creativity that was distasteful to her: she imagined a performance artist who set himself on fire regularly. POET, WRITER, PAINTER, MUSICIAN, JUGGLER, COOK, ACTOR OK, she wrote.

But Ross and other artists had a bad habit, she knew. ABSOLUTELY NO SMOKING, she wrote.

Pam answered the phone and sent the call through. It was Jean: a single woman of about fifty who kept her figure and her looks and scared hell out of men. Those who were her intellectual and tough equals were already married to equally tough women and the fellas she settled for when she was feeling broody were complete slobs whom she kicked out after a month. "So what's my interest rate?" Jean asked with no introduction. "Did the loan go through?" she demanded.

Karen stifled a laugh. "Not as good as we thought. We negotiated two points but the buy down is significant. I'd suggest you keep the loan you have, Jean." Karen could deal with Jean as she did with many men: tell it to them straight and let them figure it out. With women, she had to establish a comfort zone and suggest options. With men, she'd lay down the choices in the first two minutes, and a lot of the times, they would choose the worst option, which she'd gently but persistently steer them from. With women, after discussion of ten to fifteen minutes, the best option would be chosen. With Jean, who demanded the straightforwardness of a male, Karen just chose the best option.

Jean, who was used to the hurtling of a freight train in her business dealings, suddenly went silent. "Oh.

Thanks," she said. She rang off abruptly. Jean's big problem, Karen concluded, was that she masked her vulnerability behind a brassiness that initially attracted men, and the vulnerability scared them away. *"Be truthful," Deirdre had said.* And what about looks? She asked herself. After thirty, a guy who was obsessed with his looks was probably insincere, but MAYBE ONLY 10 LBS. OVERWEIGHT, she wrote.

"Pam—how'd you meet Mark?" Karen asked over their chicken, spinach, avocado, mandarin orange and rice salads, cheese, and Melba toast, at lunch.

"Since Kindergarten. We both went to the same church. For six years, he went to Rattlesnake Elementary, where I was."

"And when did you know you'd marry him?"

Pam considered her words carefully, weighing the information she was about to impart and whether she wanted to share it with her employer. It was a pause Karen respected because she knew how Pam had cultivated that quality in order to get ahead of her sisters, each of whom was saddled with the limited vision of people who "settle."

"I was seventeen," she said slowly, "and I knew I wanted to get out. That was the most important thing." She shook her head at the memory, desperate, at seventeen, not to be like the other Jupps. "I'd saved my money from my 4-H pigs and didn't buy a car like everybody else. I went to the Community College and stayed in the Springs at Iverson's. When it was over, I came back home—the place I didn't want to be—and worked hard that summer baling hay and kept asking what I wanted and it was not there.

"At church, one morning in July, I saw Mark, who was just about done with his English degree at Old Siwash, in Illinois, and was itching to get back. He wanted to get his law degree at Northwestern, but his dad was about tapped out. There just wasn't any money. So I don't know where it came from, but I told him: 'Mark, if you marry me and get me away from here, I'll help get you through law school.'"

"So that was the most important thing—getting out?" Karen breathed.

Pam nodded. "When I was ten, they asked us to write what we wanted to be. I was the only girl who didn't put 'Mommy' on her paper. And every other girl from my class is now a mommy; some of 'em twice over."

"What did you put down?"

Pam grinned mischievously. "Assistant to the president of a mortgage company."

That made Karen laugh so much that she dabbed her eyes. "But aren't you worried," she asked, after she'd recovered, "that Mark will find someone else?" She realized, as she said it, that she'd voiced her own fears. Don, her ex, had started with her when they were both twenty-two, fresh out of college, and she'd worked hard to help him get his real estate license while she started the mortgage company. The days were long and the work was tedious as they set out.

Unfortunately, Don became the quiescent partner: preferring to see clients who had been sent to him; not digging them up, as Karen had done. D & K Mortgage became K Mortgage, mainly; especially since Don was away in Denver, selling houses during their second year. By their third year, Don might as well have been on the moon. Their divorce was amicable: she got the house and the business and a car, half the debts, and the cat. Karen had spent the next twenty years building her own business. Although it was still called D&K, it was hers: completely.

"No," Pam said. "No; I'm not worried. I'm taking a couple of classes in English and American Literature online so I know when he makes a poetical reference and I listen. And there's the other thing." She smiled, sort of embarrassed.

"Women want a caring, sensitive partner," Karen quoted, "who has a strong body and is intelligent; able to give them the moon and stars." She smiled, and went on: "Men want a woman to be naked and bring beer."

"Sorta' like that," Pam agreed, recognizing the words they'd giggled over from the liquor store freebie a few days before.

SOMEBODY WHO WILL HELP MY BUSINESS AND UNDERSTAND HOW IMPORTANT IT IS TO ME, Karen wrote on her list. Pam had a list since she was ten. She'd found what she'd wanted.

Karen put the list away. She met Paul, a 46 year-old mortgage banker, a couple of weeks later. That was about a year ago. He's helped her expand her business and she's hired two more assistants who work full-time with Pam. I don't know if Paul and Karen will get married, but all indications are that they will.

LV.

WINTER WALK

Deirdre H. Moon

When does the New Year begin? September? October? November? January? In Fondis there will be some folks who celebrate in each of those months according to their belief systems.

I pondered this as I pulled on my treadless, old Sorrels and layered wool scarves and hats about my head. The wind chill factor dipped to minus double digits. However Mother Nature called me and I always answer.

Parts of me wanted to stay by the wood-burning stove, snuggled with a good book and a lap full of purring Merlin. Deep inside I knew I must venture forth into the chill of the day.

As I passed the donkey shed, I offered an extra flake of hay and tugged on long, winter wooly ears and gave a kiss to soft, tender noses eager for the carrots I pulled from my pocket.

The path was only a memory as I trudged through the snowy pines, my feet knowing the way no matter the season. At last I came to the ledge leading down to the West Bijou Creek. I edged along. My foot slipped and a rock skittered over the edge. Drat. New boots leapt to the top of my wish list. A light crystalline snow flittered about my chilled face.

At last I reached the creek, a frozen water line meandering through the canyon. I headed north and paused to watch a glimmer of a flicker's red feathers. It edged up a cottonwood, ratatatting and drumming out a rhythm that caught my ears in a trance.

What had Cerridwen said about flickers? *When flicker flies into your life, there will be new rhythms coming.* Cerridwen reads nature like a tarot deck.

When this courageous bird comes to you, you have the opportunity to experience bounding leaps into your spiritual growth. She always says things like that to me. I think getting up in the morning is about my spiritual growth.

Most of America celebrates January as the beginning of the new year so a flicker on my path is a good symbol. *Flickers symbolize new sensitivity and an awakening of the heart chakra.* That sounds pretty good but it also makes me a little uneasy.

I started up the creek bed as the drumming continued. *Walk in balance, Little One.* She says that whenever I'm scattered. I always say I don't do scatter and she laughs.

I stumbled on a rock, slipped and fell against snow covered rabbit brush, ending up on my back side. A shaft of sunlight twinkled through the clouds. At least this was a sandy beach area and I didn't hurt myself. I jumped to my feet, dusting off snow. I crossed the snow covered sand and paused to peer into a cave against the bank.

I heard a nicker echo back into the recesses of the earth. I clucked a sound in return, my tongue against the roof of my mouth. The snow fell now from a darkened sky and a mist swirled around the cave.

The rhythm of reverberating hooves. The drumming of the flicker. A unicorn stepped forward, looking directly in my eyes. I fumbled in my pocket and found a snippet of carrot which I offered on a flattened hand. He paused and then nibbled, soft lips tickling my palm.

He was in my head, in my brain and I heard him even as he exhaled a billowing cloud. *Do not be afraid to open your heart center. It is your mission this year. Should you choose to accept it.*

Do unicorns have a sense of humor?

I will be with you, to help you, to protect you. Just call on me.

Suddenly I was alone on the shore of the frozen winter stream, a warmth riding through my body, an exuberance inviting me into a new year. I smiled and headed back toward the yurt.

LVI.

EPIPHANY

Roger Rural

Epiphany: *(n)* 1. An epochal change in one's life; 2. A place somewhere between Damascus and Hayseed in a rural area; 3. What one might name his ninth daughter if he had only half a testament and a limited imagination.

    Charlie and Mary Jo had only been married eight years when their first child died. He fell into a cistern and drowned. He was all of four years old. The loss of a child is especially devastating; and to a couple who really hadn't known each other until then, it created shaky ground. They were still together but they did not touch each other. This led to long silences and longer looks and a lingering question that was never spoken: would they ever want to have any other children?
    My friend Susan believes that epiphanies happen to those who look for them and are ready for them. She was ready to leave her husband of seventeen years when she had an epiphany: the most sensible move she could make was no move at all. She remained.
    The early Christian church equated epiphany with the birth of Christ: a complete change from suffering to fulfillment, no matter what the circumstances. The epiphany can appear trivial, but it is intense to the person who undergoes it. Where it leads outwardly is anyone's guess; inwardly, it leads to self-discovery.
    "If you undergo an epiphany," Janice has told me, "you have to be looking for it. The signs are all there, probably from the beginning, but you need to be in a spot where they all come together." She has had her share of epiphanies over the years; each making her stronger and more self-sufficient.
    It was an odd coincidence that Charlie and Mary Jo were walking together in the country; a spur of the moment thing where he had an afternoon off work and she was willing to join him, some forty miles south and east of Denver, where they parked the car and sauntered in silence: together but not together.

"The woods were dark and close," Mary Jo told me years later, and we had to pass in front of each other to get through; to where I don't know. And it was full of a green darkness in great contrast to the sun, which beat down hard that Autumn afternoon." She smiled, almost wistfully, remembering her younger self. "We both felt, looking at it in retrospect, that if we didn't talk, we'd go mad; but neither of us could say anything."

An epiphany is a discovery, really, of the correct direction to take. It can be accidental, as in when Cheryl completely shut down the newsmagazine she owned and edited because she realized she was neglecting her youngest child, but it can never be forced.

Jeff's a real good example of why it cannot be forced. Several of us who were concerned that his drinking was excessive and destructive tried an "intervention." We hoped that he'd become sober that evening and stay sober. We offered support; we offered advice; we pointed to his failed marriage as proof of the destructive powers of alcohol; we appealed to his best instincts for caring for his three boys, and all of it came to naught when one of his friends stood up and said loudly: "Hell, Jeff, I like you drunk!" He then amended his statement to include some notes on the debilitating effects of alcohol, but the damage was done. Jeff's epiphany that night was no epiphany at all.

Five years later, his business gone to smash and no banks willing to float him a loan, his children distant and evasive when he approaches them, Jeff is still a drunk.

"I was in front," Mary Jo was saying, "and Charlie was behind me when we suddenly stumbled on a clearing that just suddenly opened up. The sun shone in it and all around was brilliant light. And in the center of the clearing were two medium size pine trees. In front of them, equally spaced, were three small seedlings, no more than eight inches high. The tallest of those seedlings was obviously dead. Its needles were brown. But next to it, two other seedlings, green and healthy, were standing tall above the earth.

"'It's us,' I told Charlie, pointing to the trees, and saying so, I drew him to sit against the other medium size tree, and everything we needed to say about having another child or two was said."

Mary Jo and Charlie were to have two other children, miles away from that clearing, which they could never find again following that afternoon. Funny thing: I now live some thirty five miles east and south of Denver, where they had their epiphany, some fifty years ago, when the roads were dirt and the signposts were few.

Funny thing: I am their second son.

LVII.

ROSE

Deirdre H. Moon

Once upon a time a bitch whelped out a litter of unwanted pups, mix-breed bastards.

"Kill 'em," he growled. "Drown 'em."

Fate stepped in and took two; a neighbor, one. The remaining pup suckled enough nourishment to survive when the bitch didn't.

The white pup with red spots learned quickly to avoid the impact of the steel toed boot, to scrounge for food, to sneak into a shed behind the house at night. She grew, abandoned but no longer abused.

One day the harsh male voice yelled again. "Thought I told ya to get rid of that scum."

The woman cowered, nodded.

The following day the pup looked curiously out of a cage in a veterinarian's office. The receptionist wandered over, smiled at the bright eyed dog. "What's she in for?"

The vet scanned a sheet of paper. "Euthanasia."

"No," the receptionist cried. "Look at her. She's a perfectly sound. Bright eyed." The vet shrugged.

"That's what they want."

"I can't keep her," the receptionist moaned. She took the young dog home that night to a houseful of five canines.

"Saved from the jaws of death," she said. "Or the prick of a needle. We'll find you a good home, little one. You need a name. Second Hand Rose." Her daughter trained the rescued dog for 4-H.

I stopped in an out of the way vet clinic, asked a few questions, got on with the receptionist, told her I wanted a border collie mix to work the flock of sheep. She said she had my dog, had been waiting for me.

I drove to her house, waited in her living room while she went outside. Dogs and children filled the room, racing about. One dog came through the back door, ignored the melee and came to me unbidden to sit on my feet. Indeed, my dog. Maybe a hybrid rose but certainly first class.

"Want to come home with me, Rose?" She followed me to the car, jumped in the passenger seat and never looked back.

Border collie body. Dingo/red heeler coloring. Harp seal eyes. A healer in every way.

Curiosity was her bane and blessing. One night when the coyotes howled, she knocked down the screen and jumped from the window, off to protect her domain. I found her quivering, her jaw broken hours later. A fine vet set her jaw. I kept Rose with me 24 hours a day so it would mend. Always she slept in her "beddie bye" at the foot of the bed.

I never did train her; trained the sheep instead. Rose became a companion instead of a worker, the kind of dog that folks stopped to talk to, that demanded attention by her presence.

Her recent lethargy seemed natural as she entered her fourteenth year. Then her breathing became labored, shallow, raspy. Called another good vet. Took her in. Blood work. X rays. Leukemia. Medication did not dull her discomfort. Only the veterinarian could help her pass easily to the other side.

My heart is an abyss of sadness un-mended by tears.

In memoriam
Rose
1990-2004

LVIII.

FAERIE CUPS

Epona Maris

The dry grass and leaves were artfully twisted together, but I still felt I would rather have milk for my cereal. It was the tail-end of winter, just before the grass turned green when my favorite dairy goat had chosen to produce her kid. I should have been blessed with an abundance of fresh milk, but I had been going through this routine for a week: I went to the goat barn each morning to milk, but the doe was dry. She would look up at me with puzzled eyes, but no explanation as to her condition.

At first, I thought it was just because her kid was drinking everything she produced, but she had only one kid. She should have had enough milk for two and to spare for me. On top of that, she was obviously getting thinner, no matter how much grain and hay I fed her. I began to suspect the real answer the morning I heard giggling when I entered the barn.

Goats make a variety of odd noises, but they don't giggle. I looked around but couldn't find the source. It hit me then: faeries. They are notorious around Fondis for nipping milk in the middle of the night, but usually a cupful would satisfy them. I had been setting out milk each night for that reason; at least I had until the goat went dry. And now they were giggling at me.

"Unfair to take without payment in return," I told the walls of the goat barn, but heard silence in return. The next morning the little gifts started to appear—decorative bits of wildland crafts like clever acorn sculptures and dried-berry necklaces. The goat remained dry and grew thinner.

I tried reasoning with them, explaining that they were endangering the source of milk, even if they didn't care how they were inconveniencing me. They just giggled, scarcely bothering to disappear as I entered the barn each morning.

I tried surprising them at their thievery in the night, but their ears are sharper than mine so I just watched them flitting off through the moonlight, the doe already drained. The final straw came the morning I found two of them sleeping in the hay: I had to dump them into the manger to get them to wake up and fly off. They barely managed to clear the windowsill, bobbing erratically through the bright sunlight.

That night, I went looking for Showelreth in the woods. I needed a faerie's perspective to figure this one out. "They're drunks," she said, looking almost human as she laughed through her fox teeth. "Moonlight on fresh milk in a faerie's cup ferments quickly."

"I am not willing to feed their habit every night except moon dark," I told her. "Besides, I thought faeries maintained the balance of nature, not drained it dry."

"Is it not the nature of an addict to take more than there is to give?" she asked in return. "Feed the doe rowan berries and I think you will see her health return." She slipped into fox form and disappeared between the trees.

Rowan is a powerful tool against negative forces, but I had no idea it could work like antabuse with faerie alcohol. They left a mess in the goat barn the first couple of nights, then left it alone. I had my milk back for my cereal and the doe regained her weight. I even went back to leaving a little cup of milk on the windowsill for them, but they wouldn't touch a drop after that.

LIX.

IMBOLC

Deirdre H. Moon

I slid down a moonbeam slap dab in the middle of the Medicine Wheel. Cerridwen laughed.

"Am I late?" I worried.

She Who Knows All let out a great guffaw.

I hate being late. It all started when I was trying to avoid Merry MultiLevel. If it's not one thing, it's another with her. Blue green algae. The latest magnets to heal everything. Some kooky mooky juice from the South Pacific. I've tried to explain to her that there is no panacea and that each person will not always respond in the same way to a product.

"Just buy a starter kit," she'd persist. "You'll feel better." I already feel great so how could I get better? Now it's transfer factor this and transfer factor that.

So, I saw Merry walking down Main Street and I slipped into the Post Office, hoping she hadn't noticed me. She had. I fumbled with my key, my back to the door, hoping to be nonchalant.

"Deirdre, I have something to tell you." Her voice grated along my aura.

Great Goddess, save me.

"Just take two of these pills with every meal. You won't believe what it will do for you."

I don't believe it.

"Merry, I'm late for a meeting." I don't tell her I'm off to the Medicine Wheel. Not only is she a multi-level freak, she's a neo-con rightie and would be sure to scold me for seeking any alternative spirituality.

"Deirdre, this won't take a sec. Just take this trial packet. Really. It doesn't cost a thing." She pulled a pack from her pocket with a dry, chubby hand.

"Gotta run, Merry." I'm impolite, I know. "A meeting. And then I have to feed the donkeys."

She frowned. "I'll call you. We'll make an appointment. There is so much that can help you."

I sprinted out of the Post Office, through the back alley that led down to the West Bijou walking trail. That's where I caught the moonbeam express to Cerridwen's.

The Lady of the Lake gave me a big hug and chuckled. She Who Knows All made a snide remark. Cerridwen welcomed me with her usual warmth. I was safe here. I looked around the circle of women and smiled.

"We are here to honor the cross-quarter day of Imbolc," Cerridwen said. "As we sense the presence of the goddess, we must look deep within our own hearts. Love yourself first so you can love another." Her rheumy old eyes shot to me. She knew I wasn't loving toward Merry. Drat.

We held hands and moonbeams shot around us in a whirl. I felt my judgments melt and disappear. I'd work on loving myself, and then facing Merry and her ilk with at least some sort of understanding if not love. Again I felt Cerridwen's eye. Okay, I'd try to be loving toward Merry.

I closed my eyes and let the beat of the drum align with my heart beat and gave thanks for the circle of women.

LX.

LOVE'S MISTAKES

Roger Rural

"...I pray you, in your letters,
When you shall these unlucky deeds relate.
Speak of me as I am; nothing extenuate...
Of one that lov'd not wisely, but too well..."
                Othello, V, ii, lns.960-963

    It all began when Clyde Fuller, owner of Fuller's Mercantile, that commercial Fondis landmark, ordered a shipment of Valentine's Day cards from his sister-in-law's cousin, a card distributor in Seattle, who needed a little extra business to tide her over. After looking at what he'd received, he understood why she needed some extra business. He couldn't return the cards, so he made the most of it, and put the cards on a stand in the front of his store under a huge sign: SHIPPER'S MISTAKE! ALL BOXES ¾ OFF!

    It was 5:55 on a snowy February night when Leonard ran in, much to the annoyance of Betsy, who'd already counted two of the three tills and was just going to start on the third. She'd been on her feet all day and although she knew Leonard had put in twelve hours on his backhoe for Stufit Construction, she still wasn't happy to see him. "Can you hurry, Leonard?" she asked.

    He gulped, nodded, grabbed some pork chops, milk, peanut butter, mayonnaise, tuna fish, and rushed her counter. He grabbed two of the pink boxes off the display, tossed them on the counter, then ran to get a roll of paper towels, a box of detergent, and some crackers.

    "That it, Leonard?" Betsy asked. "Forty three eighty six," she said as she moved to bag his groceries. He tendered a fifty; she made change. "Say hi to your mom for me, all right?" she called as he headed for the door. The time was 5:59.

    Absently she wondered if she should've asked him about the Valentine's cards he'd purchased, but it was really none of her business what went on at his house: his salary supported his mom and his five-year-old daughter, Caroline. No, Betsy reflected, that family'd had enough troubles since Caroline's mother had decided to divorce him and disappear. Maybe Leonard was finally getting over her. Betsy hoped so.

"These for my school?" Caroline asked as Leonard unbagged the groceries on the counter.

"Yup," he smiled. "I think there are twenty there—ten in each box. Should be enough. What do you say?"

The little girl headed for the stairs, the two pink boxes in hand. "Thank you, Daddy. I'll work on 'em after dinner."

"You want pork chops or tuna tonight?" his mom asked from the doorway.

"Pork chops," he said with a grin. "I'm going out to check on the animals."

"Haven't seen 'em much today," his mom remarked. "The snow's kept 'em in the barn."

"Gramma? Where do I put my name on the Valentine?" Caroline's voice called down.

"Under the writing," she called back, busying herself with a pot of green beans.

"But there's a picture under the writing!" Caroline protested.

"How about on the back?" Gramma called.

"Oh! Okay!"

So the Valentine's Day cards were distributed two days later in Mrs. Cookson's Kindergarten class, where twenty-one students chaotically pummeled and shoved one another in their eagerness to place the right card in the right lunchbag. Caroline had forgotten to get a card for the teacher, which Mrs. Cookson noticed but immediately forgave. Most had very simple sentiments:

"Bow Wow Wow! Valentine: You're Mine!"

"I'm yours—You are mine
I'm so glad you're my Valentine."

Even the kid whose hero was an all-star wrestler, and who'd gotten his cards off the Internet, sent out some simple sentiments:

"Be my Valentine, you ugly wrestler
Because my heart's an empty nester..."

But Caroline's Valentine's cards were a bit more complicated:

*"When I experienced that first kiss,
I knew an eroticism that surpassed bliss.
Our bodies joined and made one
Is as natural as the morning greeting the sun..."*

There were beautiful pen and ink illustrations accompanying each poem, showing breasts and legs. The faces were rather nondescript, but the couples looked really happy. Caroline had carefully colored some of them red.

And unfortunately, Mrs. Diamorgio, whose son Mark was Caroline's classmate, happened to look through her son's Valentine's Day cards, worried that Marky hadn't gotten as many cards as the other children had, and she called the Principal of Fondis Consolidated School, grades K-12, that night. Fortunately, he was home, and urged her to see him first thing the next morning, without calling any other parents or Mrs. Cookson, at least until he'd seen the "pornography."

Duke, editor of the Fondis Herald, *was at home that night, too; the Principal thanked his stars. "We don't need this kinda' news story," the Principal urged him. All it's gonna' do is hurt people and embarrass a lot of others." Duke concurred and rang off.*

And the Principal thought of a sophomore this year: a pimply faced wrestler named Tim, whose mother, Laura, had been a classmate of his at the same school some twenty years before: her interest in the Hains boy was obvious and obviously mistaken: he'd taken off shortly after she got pregnant. She'd gotten her GED when the boy was two. If he'd been Principal then, he wondered, would he have told her to stay home and not finish with her class?

Mrs. Diamorgio was in his office at eight o'clock that morning, brandishing the Valentine's Day card. "Just look at this!" she demanded.

He did, suppressing a desire to laugh. On the back, in careful pencil, with the G backwards, was the name: CAROLINE GOULD. The woman's figure was a bright red, which highlighted her otherwise exposed torso. She and the man were about to embrace.

"You know this was a mistake, don't you, Margaret?" he asked quietly. "If she or her dad knew exactly what this said, do you think they'd distribute them?

"But how many other children have been traumatized?" she demanded.

"Was Marky really traumatized?"

There was something about his look and tone that made her pause. He knew, as she did, that Marky had no idea there was anything wrong.

"In a small town, we all have to get along, Margaret. Raising a stink about this wouldn't do any good." He let that sink in, then added, "I'll talk with Mrs. Cookson and the other teachers and make sure this doesn't happen again. Meantime—"he put the Valentine's Day card in the desk drawer—"the less said, the better."

Duke called him later that evening. "She came around to see me," he said, "and wondered if you were doing a cover-up. I asked if she had the card so I could see it for a possible story. She said you'd taken it."

"Yup."

"End of story, then."

"Yup. Oh—you get around, Duke: You know Laura Sears? Tim Sears' mom?"

"Yeah—still living at the same place, I think."

"You know if she's seeing anyone?"

EPILOGUE

If we were "stuck," as the TV reporters put it, then Deirdre, Epona and I did not realize it in the offices of *The High Plains Rider* during "the worst snowstorm in years." We had things to do: answer the phones, do the interviews: get the information, then disseminate it.

Ephraim Calkins almost lost his life searching for two cows who'd left the herd; Matilda Brewer had a whole busload of Florida tourists sleeping in her barn; Our Holy Mother of Indiscriminate Sinning Church had a troupe of Kansas City hoop dancers entertaining the nuns. Oh—and usually late at night, this volume was completed.

"Three intrepid reporters are stuck in the offices of their newspaper in the middle of the Bijou Valley, but they refuse to give up," the television reporter boomed over pictures of the snow covering the area, "and file stories regularly in addition to helping coordinate disaster relief. Attempts to contact them have been fruitless..."

"Hey—"the voice boomed at four in the morning from the telephone receiver. "Ed Slowit from CNN here. How's it goin'?"

I looked at Epona and Deirdre, who started laughing, when I replied that we were fine and had a story to cover. I rang off.

The stranded pre-schoolers at Kutch were sleighed into the terminal at Fondis International Airport; Mrs. O'Riley's son got her and her 103 year-old younger sister to the Liberal Arts Building of the University by tractor power for dialysis; milk was delivered by helicopter fresh from Burns' Goat Farm, to children at the Hong Kong Conasupo; two sheriff's deputies sang to a herd of buffalo at Bozo's Bison Business to calm the animals down: and we covered it all!

The snow abated after three days. By the fourth day, snowshoers appeared on the streets, most of them carrying light groceries.

"Fuller's Mercantile must have reopened," I remarked, pointing to a citizen carrying a sack of flour and a bag of dog food on his back.

"Zeke damn near buried himself in the snow, just shoveling," Vera, the store manager, remarked about her seventy-two year-old husband, "But he felt it was important so people would have food and supplies, so I let him, and we're open now. We've got a sale on canned peas and twenty-five-watt light bulbs, if you want to come on down."

"We'll keep it in mind, Vera," I promised.

"I hear snowplows," Deirdre announced at one o'clock on January fifth. "The storm is over." We watched them fencing with their headlights: cut, coutre, cut. Then they'd go on to somewhere else.

"I guess we'll be going home tomorrow," I remarked needlessly as the snowplows clanged against the flagstones and sent sparks all over.

"You know it will be different?" Deirdre asked. "You've spent five days covering a disaster and becoming yourself."

"And what have I become?"

She shrugged. "That's up to you, Roger."

She pointed to a manila folder, full of our writings, bulging on the waiting room table. "All I know is that it is."

"I'll need to get to my car," I said. "It's probably buried in the snow still, outside the Fondis Lyceum."

She smiled. "Let the thoughts churn within you awhile, Roger. There will be a snowplow outside this door at seven to pick you up."

Then Deirdre settled onto her couch as Epona had earlier, and closed her eyes. I cannot remember any more. Perhaps I staggered to my own couch and fell asleep.

I awoke, a little before seven, the morning of the fifth, on a couch, alone, in the waiting area of *The High Plains Rider*, without Epona or Deirdre or a bulging manuscript on the table.

There was an impatient rap on the door. Twice, three times. I opened it and beheld a craggy veteran of many snowstorms. "You Roger Rural?" he asked.

I nodded.

"Zeke," he said, putting out his gloved hand, which I shook automatically. "I'm here to take you to the Lyceum. No one told me to. Just heard a voice last night and figured I'd do it since I've got to plow up to there this morning."

I stared at him a moment too long.

"Funny," he smiled, "This snowstorm, you got a sense of where people was and started listening to yourself or you'd die."

I nodded, sorry for doubting his faith in a voice he'd heard in his head. After all, I had been transported by faeries.

"Where do I get in?" I asked, looking at the huge yellow machine with steel plate doors parked in front of me as I closed the office front door.

"I guess you'll want to call your family," Zeke said as I made myself comfortable standing in his tiny cab among the gears. "Here's my phone."

Rachel answered. Yes, the chickens were fine; so were her Bantams and pigeons. Could I come home real soon, please? Her brother, Raul, had made her fetch firewood all week to keep the stove going, "because Daddy would've done that. And we don't have any wood left in the garage anymore. Can you come and make some more, Daddy?"

-Roger Rural

Whatever. Perhaps that was my dominant comment to Roger after being holed up during the blizzard. Don't get me wrong. The creative process was truly inspired and the faeries attended us most every waking and sleeping moment. However, I did come to realize that however much I had in common with both these remarkable human beings, 24/7 was a bit much. I live alone in my yurt on the cliffs for a reason. This divine snowstorm alerted me to the need for detachment.

A faerie tweaks my left earring and giggles in my ear. I hear her. I guess I was pouting. Life on Earth is so different. I didn't intend to be grumpy. Maybe I'll call the Womyn's Group and see if they'd like to make a big snow goddess on the cliffs west of town.

Hours before Roger would climb up on the snowplow, I spot Cerridwen ambling down the street with Edgar Rice Burro on a lead. My beloved donkey collects snow clods on his hooves and stops while Cerridwen stoops her old frame and picks snowballs from his frogs. I dash down the stairs, avoiding ice patches and hurry to meet them. Soon I'd be home again—and planning a representation of the divine feminine in snow.

-Deirdre H. Moon

I made my departure from the essay incubator before the sun rose over the snowbanks. The stone path opened unexpectedly and beckoned me home.

I knew that the faeries would be taking good care of my goats even though they were dry of milk at this season, but I wanted to check on them anyway. No sense letting the faeries get too fond of them again.

The goats were nearly as happy to see me as I filled their manger with hay. I broke a path to my cabin as the sunlight slipped along the sparkling ridge.

I was tired, in need of a bath and achingly glad to be sheltered within my own home, but I knew I had changed. I am no longer just a lone observer in this world and the possibilities are endless.

-Epona Maris